Sharper's Quest

Sharper Wade rides into Virginia City more by chance than intent. He'd heard about the Comstock Lode and the vast wealth in gold and silver that was being mined there, but Sharper's needs are limited to having enough money to eat, feed his horse and buy ammunition.

He is in town no more than an hour when he witnesses a brutal attack on a defenceless girl and her grandfather by three cowboys and steps in to help, landing himself in jail accused of murder. But he had a witness who can exonerate him and Sharper needs to find the men responsible, or lose his life. . . .

Sharper's Quest

Jay D. West

A Black Horse Western

ROBERT HALE · LONDON

© Jay D. West 2013
First published in Great Britain 2013

ISBN 978-0-7198-0919-4

Robert Hale Limited
Clerkenwell House
Clerkenwell Green
London EC1R 0HT

www.halebooks.com

All comments welcome
Oxtondel@aol.com

Typeset by
Derek Doyle & Associates, Shaw Heath
Printed and bound in Great Britain by
CPI Antony Rowe, Chippenham and Eastbourne

To Cliff and Sue
Two of the loveliest people I know

CHAPTER 1

Sharper Wade rode into Virginia City, Utah Territory.

Sharper was a drifter, had been now for over twenty years. He was never a bounty hunter, but trouble always seemed to dog him wherever he went. Not always to him, but mostly around him. Injustice and brutality were things he could not tolerate and, wherever possible, he had tried to set things to rights. But right now, all he wanted was to get King into the livery and then get himself sorted out. It had been a long and dusty ride.

Sharper had never seen so many people in his life. The city seemed to be jam-packed with miners, wagons, riders and buggies filling the main street. He'd heard the Comstock Lode, which had been discovered only a year earlier, was so rich in silver, all you had to do was sneeze and it jumped into your hand.

Tired and hungry after his last set-to in a no-name

7

town* all he wanted was some grub, a bath and a comfortable bed for the night.

He reined in outside a bustling café proudly showing a sign that read Sam's Eatery. The smell of the food was tantalizing. He dismounted and tied King to the hitch-rail, intent on entering. King sniggered, and a hoof pawed the ground.

'All right, boy. I'll sort you first,' Sharper smiled and stroked King's head.

'Tell me where the livery is, mister?' he asked a passing stranger.

'Sure ting, down three blocks, take a left and first buildin' on the right.'

'Thanks, sure is an accent you have there,' Sharper commented.

'You'll hear a lot of strange accents here, mister, I'm Irish.'

Sharper nodded and thanked the man again. Remounting, he walked King down to the livery. The liveryman, a rotund bald man in his fifties, took a shining to King.

'Mighty fine beast, mister,' he said.

'He sure is,' Sharper said. 'Best feed you got an' a comfortable stall for the night. What's the charge?'

'Well, with barley and oats and a good rub down to get rid o' some of that there trail dust, I reckon

* See *Hell Riders*, (Robert Hale Limited, 2001).

a dollar fifty will cover it,' the man said.

A dollar more than Sharper was used to paying, but this was Virginia City.

'OK.' He handed over the money. 'I'll be back in the mornin',' he said, and left the livery, his stomach rumbling.

He made his way back to the eatery, stepped up on the boardwalk and dusted himself down as best he could before entering. The name Eatery was an understatement, Sharper thought. He looked round at the opulence of the establishment. Crystal chandeliers hung from the ceiling; there was a deep red carpet on the floor and every table, of which he reckoned there were twenty or so, had a white tablecloth on it. The chairs were covered in a red velvet that matched the carpet, and the walls had a fancy patterned wallpaper, mirrors and paintings hanging everywhere.

It wasn't only the place that was opulent; the customers were, too. Around twenty people, Sharper reckoned, evenly split between men in fancy duds and women in dresses the like of which he'd never seen. The place dripped money and Sharper felt slightly ill at ease. Faces turned towards him, noting his dust covered denims, trail-worn boots, sweat soaked shirt and bandanna and the crumpled Stetson, which he quickly removed. It was the low-slung Colt at his side that folks were mostly wary of, though his stubble-covered face didn't help matters much. People looked away, avoiding eye contact, but Sharper noticed their look of distaste as they started to chatter once again, trying to ignore the stranger.

A large man approached him. He was wearing a brilliant-white apron, a red shirt with a string tie, and a black waistcoat. 'Help you, mister,' he said.

'Some vittals an' a coffee would be mighty welcome,' Sharper said.

The big man hesitated slightly, before answering, 'No offence, but you got the means, mister?'

Sharper slowly banged his Stetson on one leg and a shower of dust fell to the red carpet. He ran his fingers through his long, straggly hair, and gave the man a steely-eyed look. 'I got the means, mister,' he replied.

As Sharper's eyes drilled into him, the man said, jovially, 'Then I got the vittals.' He led the way to a table set in the far corner of the room. Sharper noticed the ladies put handkerchiefs to their noses as he passed, and he grinned.

The big man introduced himself: 'Sam's the name,' he said, 'what can I get you?'

'Steak,' Sharper replied, 'the bloodier the better, an' whatever veg you have.'

'Sure thing. We got potatoes and greens and gravy, too, if'n you want.'

'Sounds good to me, an' coffee. Lots of coffee.'

Sharper noticed a newspaper on the chair

10

beside him and picked it up. The *Territorial Enterprise*, the banner displayed. One story caught his attention, written by a Samuel Clemens. Seems Clemens was robbed on his way into Virginia City; thieves stole all his money and a three hundred-dollar gold watch.

Sharper whistled silently. Hell, even a reporter has a gold watch worth more than anything he had ever owned in his entire life. But it seems it was a practical joke played on Mr Clemens by his friends so he'd have a story to write, and by the way he told the story, Mr Clemens didn't find it funny.

The coffee arrived, hot and strong. Sharper felt all the trail dust in his dry throat wash away as the liquid hit his belly. The steak was the biggest Sharper had ever seen; it filled the large white plate, overlapping it on one side and there were mashed potatoes and greens, too, piled like a mountain and covered in gravy.

'Thought you might manage that,' a beaming Sam said as he delivered the food.

'Watch me,' Sharper said, and tucked in. Fifteen minutes later, he was sitting in front of an empty plate. He'd drunk a whole pot of coffee and his stomach was as full as he could ever remember.

'Mighty fine steak, mister,' Sharper said as Sam cleared the table.

'We got the best apple pie this side of the Sierras,' Sam said.

'Hell, I couldn't eat another thing,' Sharper replied. 'What's the damage?' he asked.

'Five dollars, all in,' Sam replied.

'A mite more than I'm used to payin',' Sharper said, 'but worth every penny. I guess everything in this town is two to three times more than any place I've ever been.'

'Virginia City is a boom town, mister. Reckon they got over a hundred million dollars worth of silver and gold outa that Lode so far, an' that's only scratching the surface. Reckon we got over nine thousand people living here now, miners from all over the world, some of 'em have pretty strange habits, too.'

'I need a room for the night, and a bath and shave,' said Sharper, changing the subject. 'Recommend anywhere?'

'Sure, Harvey's, the barber down the street aways, and opposite is a hotel. Cost you three dollars for the shave and bath, and six for the room.

Sharper whistled. 'Seems a man can run out of money pretty damn quick here,' he said.

'A man can make plenty, too,' Sam said.

Sharper handed over the five dollars, thanked the man and left. Once outside, he paused; the cool air of early evening was a welcome relief to the heat in the eatery. He stood on the boardwalk, pulled out a cheroot and inhaled deeply. The sky was a light purple colour with stars faintly pushing through the fading sunlight. Main Street was still full of traffic; fancy rigs of all sizes, salt wagons, lumber wagons, Conestogas by the dozen. It seemed like it would never end.

Sharper walked back to the livery, collected his saddle-bag and gunny sack and set off to Harvey's. His eyes already weary, he knew he'd sleep long that night.

'Shave, mister?' A small slim man with a full head of hair and moustache like a walrus asked him.

'That, a haircut an' a bath,' Sharper said.

'That'll be four dollars.'

'Sam said three!'

'Hell, OK, three then. Sit yourself down.'

Covered in a red, white and blue sheet, Sharper closed his eyes and relaxed. Harvey prattled on and Sharper grunted now and then, while the barber first shaved, then cut his hair.

'OK, bath'll be five minutes. Follow me, mister,' Harvey said, after he'd removed the sheet and brushed the pile of greasy hair on the floor to one side.

Sharper looked at himself in the mirror, then rubbed a rough hand over his chin and cheeks. 'Mighty fine shave you give, mister,' he said.

'Heck, I could shave a possum blindfolded,' Harvey grinned.

He led the way through to the backroom, where a tin tub was being filled by a small girl with long, black hair.

'Soo Lee will take care of you now,' Harvey said, and returned to the shop front.

Sharper stood and stared at the girl, then at the tin tub, which was now full and had them fancy bubbles in it.

'Er, ma'am,' Sharper began, 'I need to get me undressed now so if—'

'Yes, please,' the girl said. 'I take care of you. Soo Lee wash your back.'

'All due respect, ma'am, I'd rather you didn't. In fact I'd prefer to be left alone.'

The girl's face dropped. 'You no want me wash you?'

'No thanks, ma'am.'

Her head sank further.

'No offence, I just feel a mite, you know, uncomfortable.'

A crestfallen Soo Lee bowed, then left the bathroom.

Sharper started to undress, making sure his gunbelt was within easy reach. Buck naked, he stepped into the tub. The water was hot, but bearable as he sank his weary limbs into it. Cheroot clenched between his teeth, he closed his eyes, feeling the trail weariness fade from his bones.

Then Harvey disturbed his peace and quiet.

'You sure 'bout Soo Lee, mister? She's powerful upset out there.'

Sharper opened one eye.

'All she does is scrub your back. You'll feel better for it,' Harvey added.

Sharper looked down at the bath water, the bubbles covered him, with just his knees poking though. 'OK,' he said. 'Send her in.'

Soo Lee came in seconds later. 'You lean forward, please,' she said.

Sharper sat up and rested his arms on the side of the tub. Soo Lee got to work. He had to admit to himself that it sure felt good. Soo Lee was using a cloth and carbolic and rubbed his skin hard until he felt the aches and pains from a long ride dissipate. She stopped scrubbing and poured hot water over his neck and back; then he felt her hands on his shoulders, her fingers and thumbs moving in a circular motion towards his neck.

'Man, that sure feels good,' Sharper had to say. He closed his eyes as he felt the stiffness gradually fade away.

Soo Lee finished her neck massage. 'You feel good now? she asked.

'Ma'am, I never felt better.' Sharper leaned back in the tub, the cheroot still clamped between his teeth.

'Glad you OK,' Soo Lee said, and walked to the front of the tub, picking up a large white towel, which she placed on a chair.

'When you ready,' she said.

Sharper opened his eyes to look at the woman. No, girl, he thought; she looked even younger than he'd first thought. 'Thank you kindly, ma'am,' he said. Then he noticed the complete absence of the foaming bubbles! He sat bolt upright and covered his privates with both hands.

'Me no look, no worry,' Soo Lee said, with a smile on her face.

Sharper, for all his years and experience, felt himself blush. Damn the carbolic, he thought. Soo Lee bowed and left Sharper to his own devices.

An hour later, dressed in clean clothes and feeling like a million dollars, which, he thought, you'd need to live in a place like this, Sharper paid Harvey, tipping him an extra dollar, and another for Soo Lee, who was nowhere to be seen, and walked across the street to the hotel. Dodging the traffic was no easy task. If anything, the street was even busier than when he'd arrived. He stepped up on to the boardwalk on the far side of the street to see Soo Lee. But she was not alone. An old man, a long pigtail hanging down his back, was holding on to her arm and they had been stopped by three drunken cowboys.

'Well, lookee here, boys, seems we got ourselfs a Chinee whore! Ain't he a bit old for you, darlin'?

You need a real man, don't look like this ol' Chink could keep his pecker up at all. You even got a pecker, ol' man?' the cowboy laughed.

'He my grandfather. Please, leave us alone,' Soo Lee pleaded.

The cowboy stepped forward and shoved the old man away. He fell off the boardwalk and into the dirt of the busy street. Soo Lee let out a scream and tried to get to the old man, but the cowboy grabbed her arm. 'You an' me's gonna have some fun, gal,' he snarled.

One of the other men bellowed, 'Hell, Bart, the ol' man here's got hisself a pigtail!' He stepped off the boardwalk and, taking out a hunting knife, grabbed the pigtail and sliced it off.

Soo Lee gasped.

'OK, let the girl go,' Sharper said, stepping towards the men.

'Mind your business, friend,' one of the men said.

'This is my business, and I ain't no friend.' Sharper placed his saddle-bag and gunny sack on the boardwalk, not taking his eyes off the three men.

Bart, the cowboy who had grabbed hold of Soo Lee, roughly pushed her aside. She landed next to her grandfather, who was struggling to stand up.

'So what you gonna do 'bout it?' Bart sneered.

'Soo Lee, help your father up,' Sharper said.

'He my grandfather,' Soo Lee replied as she

17

stepped off the boardwalk.

'I said, what you gonna do 'bout it?' Bart rasped.

'Go on your way, you men, and don't try any-thing you might well regret,' Sharper said, his tone icy cold.

The three men laughed.

'And jus' what do you think you're gonna do, stranger?' Bart stepped forward menacingly, his right hand moving slowly towards his six-gun.

'Take him, Bart!' one his companions said, knowing how fast Bart was on the draw.

'No need,' said Bart.

That was the last sound Sharper heard.

Behind him, Sharper had enough time to hear a footfall, then blackness overtook him and he slumped to the ground.

'Nice timing, Will,' Bart said.

Soo Lee was struggling to get her grandfather to his feet when Bart stepped forward, took out Sharper's six-gun, and fired two shots. He then placed the gun in Sharper's hand. Soo Lee screamed as the first bullet slammed into her grandfather's chest, the force of the .45 slug ramming him backwards into the dirt. The second slug ripped into Soo Lee's back as she went to him.

It was a strange scene. The two dead Chinese lying in the dirt didn't even get a second glance from the many people who passed by.

The four men, still laughing, walked off.

CHAPTER 2

When Sharper eventually came to, it was to see a rough brick ceiling illuminated by a strong sun. It took him a few seconds to regain his senses, wondering where the hell he was.

'So, you awake now?' a voice Sharper didn't know asked.

Sharper tried to sit up, but the throbbing in his head made him wince and lie down again.

'Where am I?' he asked.

'Right where you deserve to be,' the voice said.

'This a guessing game?' Sharper said, but the sarcasm was lost on the man.

'You're in jail, mister, an' days off from being hanged.'

'What!' Sharper sat up this time. 'What the hell you talkin' about?'

'Don't try playin' a dumb ass with me, mister. We got your gun, and we got us witnesses to the killin's, too.'

'What killin's?' Sharper asked.

'You'll find out tomorrow at the trial,' the deputy sneered. 'Oh, by the way, the hangin's the day after.'

'Nice to know there's gonna be a fair trial,' Sharper said, sarcastically. 'Who are these so-called witnesses?' he asked.

'You'll find out as soon as the sheriff gets in,' the deputy answered and then left the cell block, closing the door behind him. Sharper heard the lock click.

His senses became more and more focused. He'd obviously been in the cell overnight. The sunlight filtering through the barred window was strong and bright. He shook his head, and a wave of pain and nausea swept over him briefly as he tried to regain his thoughts and remember the events of the previous evening. Gradually, his memory returned. He'd been slugged harder than he thought. The vision of the sneering cowboy, and the two shots he thought he had heard filled his mind, and then nothing. He laid back on the cell cot and closed his eyes, not to sleep, but to focus on the faces he'd seen; the three cowboys and the briefest of glances at the fourth.

He locked them in his memory. And then sleep did take him.

*

Sharper was being roughly shaken.

'Come on, wake up, got some grub for you.'

Slowly, Sharper's eyes opened and he peered into the face of a grey-haired man, with a neat moustache.

'Beans, fat-belly, bread and coffee,' the man said.

Sharper sat up and lowered his legs to the floor. His head felt as if a buffalo had stomped on it.

'What's your name, stranger?' the man asked.

'Sharper,' came the reply.

'I'm Sheriff Bill Prady. Seems like you got yourself a witness here, Mr Sharper.'

'Just Sharper, folks call me Sharper.'

'Well, Sharper, seems Harvey saw the whole thing.'

'The barber?' Sharper asked.

'Yup. Says you tried to stop three men from messin' with the Soo Lee girl and her grandfather when you were slugged from behind by a fourth man.'

Sharper wordlessly reached for the coffee and took a mouthful. It seemed to revitalize him instantly. He quickly finished the mug and wiped his lips. 'Any more coffee?' he asked.

'Sure,' the sheriff answered. 'Silas, bring the coffee pot through.'

A morose deputy came through holding the coffee pot and poured some into Sharper's outstretched mug.

Sharper received it gratefully and this time took small sips. 'So I can go?' Sharper asked.

'Well, we still got witnesses to say you did the shooting. Your gun had been fired; there were three slugs missing in the chamber and the Smith & Wesson was in your hand when I found you.'

'Sheriff,' Sharper looked at the man steadily, 'if I shot those two Chinese, how come I got me slugged?'

'Coulda been a bystander, you know, someone making sure you didn't escape.' It was the deputy who spoke up.

'And these witnesses,' Sharper asked, 'who are they?'

'Well, we got ourselves a problem there,' the sheriff replied. 'Seems they plumb disappeared.'

'So the only witness you got is Harvey, and he says it weren't me?'

'That's about the size of it,' the sheriff replied.

'Did Harvey recognize any of the four men?' Sharper asked.

'Mister, there are nigh on nine thousand folks living in this here city.'

'We got us more saddle-bums and no-good immigrants arriving every day here trying to get rich – by fair means or foul,' the deputy added.

Sharper reached out and took the plate of food. He wolfed down the beans and fat-belly, wiping the plate with the bread. 'That feels better,' he commented. 'I got the faces of three of the men in my head, I aim to track 'em down, Sheriff.'

The deputy looked a little sheepish as he said: 'Sorry I was a tad mean to you earlier, mister, but then you was guilty of murder.'

Sharper didn't respond. 'Is my gear here?' he asked.

'Sure, your gun-rig, war bag and saddle-bag are in the front office. Come on through,' the sheriff said making his way out of the cell block. 'Silas,' he called out, 'go get Doc James. Better check out Sharper's head afore we let him go.'

'Sure thing, Sheriff.'

'I don't need no doc,' Sharper said.

'That's as maybe, but for my peace of mind . . .' the sheriff left the sentence unfinished.

Doc James arrived within minutes and proceeded to examine Sharper's head. 'Looks to me like you need a coupla stitches there, young fella.'

Sharper sighed. 'That really necessary, Doc?' he asked.

'Not at all,' the doc replied. 'We can leave the wound open to infection; you might get flies laying eggs in it while you sleep. 'Course, there's always the chance of blood poisoning; you can take your pick, mister.'

'OK, OK, I get the message,' Sharper replied.

'Might sting a bit,' the doc said.

'Let's get this over with, shall we?' Sharper said, through gritted teeth.

'Just gonna clean the wound up some,' the doc said, and he dabbed some brown liquid on the open wound, which stung like all hell. He threaded his needle and got to work. 'Maybe three stitches I think,' he said, more to himself than anyone else.

Within five minutes he'd finished.

'There, that should hold it.' He took out a small bandage and proceeded to wrap it round Sharper's head. 'There, all done. Come back and see me in a week an' I'll take the stitches out.'

'Thanks, Doc.' Sharper pulled his Stetson on and stood up.

'Now I got me some poisoning to sort out,' the doc said.

'Poisoning?' Sharper inquired.

'I keep telling the miners not to drink the water near the mines, but they keep on doing it. We found traces of gold, silver, and worst of all, small quantities of arsenic. Not enough to kill a man outright, but if you drink enough of it – well, it don't do a body any good.'

'You said "we," Doc, how many of you are there?'

'Hell, we got six physicians here in Virginia City. There may be a gold and silver boom, but there sure is a medical boom to go with it,' the doc laughed to himself.

The sheriff handed Sharper his gun-rig, which he quickly put on, having felt naked without it. 'Your war bag and saddle-bag are over there,' the sheriff pointed to the corner of the office.

'Well I guess thanks are due, Sheriff, Doc, Deputy. I aim to find those fellas and bring 'em in.'

The steely look in Sharper's eyes left no doubt in the men's minds that this man was not a person to fool with.

Sharper left the sheriff's office and made his way to the hotel he had intended to check into the previous night.

The clerk, a middle-aged, pompous-looking character, with a fat belly and a red, sweaty complexion, looked down his nose at the newcomer.

'Help you, mister?'

Sharper sized up the man in an instant. 'Yeah, a room.'

'Prices start at five dollars a night,' the clerk said in an offhanded manner. 'In advance.'

Sharper slapped twenty-five dollars down on the counter. 'Five nights to start with,' he said in a gruff voice.

The clerk coughed as he scooped up the money. 'Certainly, sir,' he said and reached behind him for a room key and handed it over.

Sharper signed the register, using a false name.

'Top of the stairs, third door on your left.

25

Number twelve.'

Sharper picked up his gear and made for the stairs.

'Hey, mister,' the clerk called out, 'aren't you the guy who killed those—'

Sharper spun round to face the man, the steely look in his eyes made the clerk take an involuntary step back.

'I didn't mean—' the clerk went on.

Sharper turned back and climbed the stairs.

Unlocking the door to his room, he placed his war bag on a small table, hung his saddle-bag and Stetson over the brass bedstead and sat on the edge of the bed and surveyed the room. It was plusher than he was used to. There were two rugs either side of the bed, a wardrobe and dressing table. Another small table housed a wash bowl, jug, a bar of lyle and a small towel.

There were curtains across the window and several framed pictures adorned the wallpapered walls. Ever vigilant, Sharper checked underneath the bed, only to find a piss pot. Hell, they thought of everything here.

Stripping off his leather vest and cotton shirt, he unbuckled his gun-rig and hung it near his saddle-bag, then poured some water into the bowl and splashed his face and upper body with the tepid water. Drying himself off, he crossed to the window and slightly parted the curtains to take a quick look at the street. Although just off Main Street, it was a busy area. He could see Harvey's place across from the hotel. Next to that was a gun store. In fact, the whole side of the street was crammed with small businesses; a milliner's, dry-goods, a furniture store and what looked like a miner's supply shop, the window being filled with pickaxes, shovels and a wheelbarrow at centre stage. There was a small eatery at the end of the block that didn't look as fancy – and hopefully was not as pricey – as the place he'd eaten at the previous night.

Taking a fresh shirt from his war bag, Sharper dressed and re-hitched his gun-belt. Time to get the lay of this burg, he thought. Once outside, he bought a new copy of the *Territorial Enterprise* and made his way to the eatery. He sat at a table in the window, ordered coffee and opened up the paper. Seems this Samuel Clemens wrote under the name of Mark Twain and was the leading light in the *Enterprise*. Sharper read several small articles, and found a story by Twain which made him smile. 'The Celebrated Jumping Frog of Calaveras County'.

Then a small headline caught his attention. The story had obviously been written before Sharper had been cleared. 'Man Shoots Chinese Dead in Street' the headline proclaimed, and went on to describe the incident leading up to Sharper's arrest. It failed to mention, however, that he'd been released. It went on to describe him as a 'saddle-bum', who'd just ridden into Virginia City, and the 'sort of man that needed to be hanged for his dastardly act as a deterrent to others'.

Fortunately, Sharper's name wasn't mentioned. He finished his coffee, folded the paper and left a quarter on the table as he left.

Now to visit Harvey.

He found the old barber brushing black hair into the corner of the shop, before shovelling it up into a sack. 'Howdy, mister,' Harvey smiled. 'Good to see you up, out and about.'

'Good to be out, thanks to you,' Sharper said and held out a hand.

Harvey gripped it. 'Never did get your name, friend,' Harvey said.

'Wade,' Sharper replied, 'Sharper Wade and I'm obliged to you, Harvey.'

'Hell, only told what I saw.'

'You seen those fellas before?' Sharper asked.

'Seen a couple of them, but no names or anything,' Harvey replied.

'Didn't look like miners to me,' Sharper said.

'Nope. Probably claim hustlers.'

'Claim hustlers?' Sharper asked.

'Yeah, tricksters. They stake a claim on the hills and then try and sell it to any unsuspecting prospector. Makes for a lot of money and a lot of disgruntled prospectors.'

'Well I reckon they must live here someplace,' Sharper said after a thoughtful pause.

'This is a big city, Mr Wade.'

'I got all the time in the world. They tried to frame me for murder, an' I ain't letting that pass.'

'I tended Soo Lee,' Harvey said, his voice thick with emotion. 'She sure was a sweet gal.'

'I aim to bring her killers to justice,' Sharper stated.

'The Chinese community are pretty het up at the moment, Sharper. I should watch your back. Could be they figure it's a cover up and that you and me are in cahoots.'

'Another good reason for finding these fellas, then,' Sharper replied.

'Well, good luck with that. I'll keep my eyes and ears open. Someone's bound to know something an' you know how folks like to gossip with their barber!' Harvey gave a sly wink.

'Keep me posted, Harvey. I'm at the hotel yonder for the next five days at least.'

'Will do. You take care now,' Harvey added as the two men shook hands again.

Sharper's next port of call was to visit King and make sure he was OK and pay for another four nights, minimum. When he arrived at the livery, a young ostler was rubbing down his horse. King immediately snorted and pawed the ground as

Sharper approached him. He patted the animal's rump, 'Howdy, partner,' he said softly.

'This your horse, mister?' the ostler asked.

'Sure is. You're doing a fine job there, son.' Sharper said.

'Thank you, mister, he's a fine animal.'

'Need to extend my stay here in Virginia City, maybe another four nights,' Sharper said.

'Mr Sam, the boss, will take care of that,' the ostler said, and called out for his boss.

'Quit your bellowin', boy. I ain't deaf!' came a gruff response.

'Mister here needs his horse stablin' for longer, Mr Sam.'

'Oh, it's you.' Sam Russell appeared out of the gloom.

'Yeah, it's me,' Sharper replied in the same off-hand manner. 'Stayin' longer than I planned; maybe another four days. Here's six dollars for King's stablin'.'

'You under arrest?' Sam asked.

'Nope.'

'Not sure I want a killer's horse here,' Sam stated bluntly.

'Mister,' Sharper said, his voice as hard as iron, 'I didn't kill those two people. Harvey saw the whole thing. You go see him if you don't believe me. But I warn you, I don't take too kindly to be called a liar!'

'Only repeatin' what I heard, mister,' Sam said.

'Well you heard wrong,' Sharper grated.

'OK, mister, I'll take your word for it,' Sam said.

'I'll be checking King so you better take good care of him,' Sharper said and thrust the six dollars into Sam's hand.

'Don't you worry none, mister,' the young ostler piped up. 'I'll take good care of him.'

Sharper grunted. Turning back to King, he patted the animal and stroked his face and King nudged him in return. 'You take care, boy,' he said, then to the young ostler, 'I'll be back in the morning. What's your name, boy?'

'Arnie, sir.'

'OK, Arnie, be seeing you.'

With that Sharper left the livery.

The shot rang out like a thunderclap.

Sharper threw himself to the ground, drawing his Smith & Wesson as he fell. Another shot boomed out, and Sharper lost consciousness.

CHAPTER 3

Invitations had been sent out for the funeral of Soo Lee and her grandfather.

There were two types; one white, for Soo Lee, and one pink for her grandfather. Tradition had it that, living past eighty, as Chen Lee was, was a feat worth celebrating not mourning. The congregation at the wake was split in two; half wearing black, for Soo Lee, the other half, white trimmed with either pink or red for Chen Lee. White envelopes containing money were placed on both bodies, which were shrouded in white. The Chinese community was close knit and there were no white people present. Even Harvey had not been invited, but he stood outside, his hat in his hands, head bowed, as he paid his own respects. Life in Virginia City carried on as normal. After all, it was only a Chinese funeral.

Although gunfire was a part of normal activity in

a city with so many itinerants and ne'er-do-wells, the two shots that rang out early that morning attracted more attention than usual, given the early hour of the day. Instinctively, Harvey had ducked at the first shot, and had raised himself off his haunches just as the second shot was fired. It was close by, Harvey reckoned, but he could see nothing untoward on the street.

Then out of the corner of his eye, he saw a man emerging from a side alley, by the livery stables. He was carrying a rifle. Harvey couldn't see the man's face, or the make of rifle, but the man sure was in a hurry. Harvey moved as quickly as his old legs would carry him and entered the alleyway. He saw Sam and the young lad he employed standing over a body. As he approached he saw the body was Sharper.

'What the hell happened here?' Harvey almost shouted.

'Beats me, Harve,' Sam said. 'Fella checked his hoss, next thing we hear the shots.'

'Arnie,' Sam turned to the young ostler, 'go fetch the doc, pronto.'

'He alive?' Arnie asked.

'Sure is. Bleedin' a lot, but he's still breathin',' Harvey said. 'Now git!'

Sharper let out a low, deep groan.

'Keep still, son,' Harvey said. 'The doc's on his way.'

33

Within minutes, Doc James arrived, beaded in sweat. 'OK, let me get at him,' he panted. The doc kneeled down, opened up his black bag and took out some cloths. He started dabbing at Sharper's head.

'Easy, Doc,' Sharper winced, 'that's a tad sore there.'

'Goddamn,' the doc said, 'you must be the luckiest fella alive. Bullet's creased your skull, another quarter-inch and we'd be carting off your body to Boot Hill yonder.'

'You get a look at him, Sharper?' Harvey asked.

'Not a sight,' Sharper replied. 'First slug hit me. Lucky it did; I fell as the second shot was fired, clean missed me.'

'Mister,' Sam said, 'you been in town less'n twenty-four hours. Two people been kilt and you been slugged and shot. Must be some kinda record.'

'One I'd rather not have,' Sharper said, sitting up.

'Hold still there, cowboy. You need some more stitchin' on your noggin afore you can leave.'

The doc carefully threaded a needle and set to work. 'You should be used to this by now,' he joked. Finishing up the sutures, the doc fished out a bandage and proceeded to wrap it around Sharper's head. 'Now, you keep this on for a few days – don't want that wound infected. And try and not get shot or slugged or anything in the mean-time,' the doc said as he packed his bag and stood up.

Slowly, Sharper got to his feet. He felt dizzy and almost fell, but Harvey grabbed an arm and helped steady him. 'Come on back to my place,' he said. 'You could use a good strong coffee, an' no one makes stronger coffee than I do.'

Reluctantly, Sharper allowed himself to be led away.

'You sure you hit him?' Bart Sampson said, as Ben Doyle entered their cabin.

'Sure as eggs is eggs,' Ben replied. 'Saw him go down after the first shot.'

'He's the only one can finger us,' Clem Watson added unnecessarily.

'Will, you'll have to recce the town seein' as how you're the only one he didn't see. If'n that fella ain't dead, we need to know.' Bart looked at Will, who nodded.

'Makes sense, I guess,' Will replied. 'Might take a whiles. Where did you shoot him, Ben?'

'In the head, dummy,' Ben replied.

'I mean where in town, you doosie!'

'Oh, as he was leaving the livery.'

'OK, I'll stable my horse and see what I can find out. If'n he's alive, you want me to kill him?' Ben asked.

'Sure. Yeah, kill the sonuver,' Bart said, smirking. 'Serves him right fer interfering in stuff that don't concern him.'

Will finished his coffee and lit up a quirly, drawing deeply, holding the smoke in his lungs before exhaling. He checked his Colt, leaving the chamber under the hammer empty, and re-holstered it. He then grabbed his Winchester and made sure it was fully loaded. Finally, he unsheathed his ten-inch Bowie knife kept on his belt at his back, and looked at the cold, hard, razor-sharp blade. A cruel smile broke out on his face as he stared at his reflection on the blade. Then, slowly, he re-sheathed it. 'I'm ready,' was all he said.

'Here,' Bart said. 'Take my Stetson; that there thing you wear ain't gonna keep the sun off'n your face. Besides, marks you out.'

Reluctantly, Will had to agree and donned the offered hat. With that, he left the cabin and saddled up, put his Winchester in the saddle scabbard and mounted his horse. 'Soon as I've any news I'll be back. Best you three don't come into town until I return. Be seein' ya.' He spurred the paint on and rode into town.

Sharper's head was pounding like an Indian war drum. His vision was slightly blurred, but getting better and all he wanted to do was sleep.

But Doc James had warned Harvey to keep him awake for as long as possible. He wasn't sure whether Sharper had concussion or not, so Harvey kept talking and pouring coffee, adding a little whiskey on the quiet. '. . . So that's why ol' Sam called it the Metropolitan Livery Stables,' Harvey concluded.

Sharper hadn't been listening to a word Harvey had said, just the end of the last sentence. He was spared asking what the hell he was talking about when Sheriff Bill Prady came in. 'How you feelin', son?' Brady asked.

'Like a horse kicked hell outa my head,' Sharper replied.

Harvey poured coffee for the sheriff, who took a sip. 'Mighty perky coffee there, Harvey.'

'Puts hairs on your chest, Bill,' Harvey grinned.

'To business now,' Prady said. 'You any idea who coulda taken a potshot at you?'

'Sheriff, I've been in town less than twenty-four hours. Apart from you and Harvey here, oh, and Sam over at the livery, I don't know anyone else. I figure it's one of the fellas that killed Soo Lee and her grandfather. Got to be.'

'Makes sense,' Prady agreed. 'You're the only one who can identify them.'

'Only three of them, Sheriff. I didn't see who slugged me from behind.'

'You better lay low for a while, son,' Prady said at

last. 'Me an' Silas'll do some investigatin' an' see what we can discover. Somebody musta seen something.'

'I ain't layin' anywhere, Sheriff,' Sharper said. 'I aim to find these killers and bring 'em to justice, not hide away somewhere.'

'Wish I'd got a good look at 'em,' Harvey said. 'All I saw was a brown derby.'

'A brown derby?' Sharper said. 'There many o' them around town, Sheriff?'

'Well, they ain't that common, but there's a few, I reckon. You remember anything else, Harvey, in that addled brain o' yours?'

Harvey was silent for a few moments. If you could hear a man thinking, this would be the time. Suddenly, Harvey's face came alight.

'Hot dang!' Harvey shouted. 'The man I saw leaving the alley after the shootin' was wearing a brown derby!'

'Don't s'pose you got his name an' address, did ya, Harvey?' the sheriff asked caustically.

It took a few moments for Harvey to realize the sheriff was joshing him.

'You got a place here, Harvey, that I can bed down in?' Sharper asked.

'Sure, that's no problem, stay as long as you like,' Harvey said, glad of the company.

'OK, thanks. I gotta get back to the hotel and grab my gear,' Sharper said.

'I'll get that for ya,' Harvey said.

'Thanks, Harvey, but I need to set the room up. I figure if it is those fellas, soon as they find out I ain't dead I'll be having a visitor.'

'Smart thinkin',' Harvey said. 'I'll get some vittals on the go fer when you get back.'

'Me an' Silas'll do the rounds now,' Sheriff Prady said, 'see if'n we find any brown derbys.'

Sharper made his way back to the hotel. With his Stetson pulled down as low as he could manage, most of the bandage was hidden, so he attracted little attention.

He located his room from outside and worked out how he could leave by the window. His room faced the side alley so, with luck, he could leave without anyone seeing him.

Entering the foyer, he noticed the clerk wasn't at his station. He rang the bell, and the seedy little man came from the inner office.

'Room key,' Sharper said without preamble.

The clerk, still wearing a haughty expression, took the key from the key board and handed it over without a word.

Sharper quickly made his way up the stairs to his room. Taking out his pistol – it paid to be wary – he unlocked the door and pushed it wide open. He scanned the room quickly, it was empty and, after closer inspection, saw that none of his gear had been moved.

Sharper re-holstered his pistol and set to work. First he arranged the bolster under the bedclothes to make it look as if someone was asleep. It didn't look too convincing but he was sure that if anyone did come into the room intent on killing him, it wouldn't be in broad daylight. He left his saddle-bag draped over the headboard and grabbed his war bag.

Now for the tricky bit.

Tying the war bag to his belt, Sharper opened the sash window and looked down. He reckoned he was fifteen or so feet from the ground, but there was a small wooden ledge about halfway down. If he could get to that, the drop to the ground would be no more than six or seven feet.

Easing his legs through the window, Sharper gripped the windowsill firmly, managed to pull the window most of the way down, and then lowered his body over the side. Looking down, he was about two feet from the protruding ledge. Taking a deep breath, Sharper let go of the windowsill and dropped like a stone. He landed on the ledge and got his fingers into the clapboard facing to prevent himself falling backwards.

Breathing heavily, his head still a little dizzy, he looked down into the alley. It was empty, but he could see folks walking past on the main street. He just hoped none of them had noticed him.

Turning sideways, Sharper knelt as low as he could go – this would be the really tricky part. He needed to grab hold of the ledge to prevent himself falling to the ground. Although only about seven feet, it was high enough to maybe break a leg or ankle, and that was the last thing he needed. Reaching down, he felt the rough wood of the ledge. Getting his palms flat on the ledge, he eased his legs over the side and, arm muscles bulging, lowered himself over the edge and hung there, sweat pouring down his face and soaking into his shirt.

Taking another deep breath, Sharper let go and dropped to the dry, sandy ground. As he landed, he bent his legs to absorb some of the impact and rolled to one side. The ground was much softer than he'd thought and, standing up, he brushed the loose sand from his clothes and smiled, relieved he hadn't broken anything.

CHAPTER 4

Will Strange rode straight to the livery and bedded his horse down. 'Mighty fine looking stallion you got there,' he said.

'Sure is,' Sam replied. 'What can I do fer ya, mister?'

'Stable my mount for a coupla days,' Will said, still staring at the horse. 'Arab?' he asked.

'Most definitely,' Sam answered. 'Finest horse I ever had here.'

'You think the owner might be willing to sell him?' Will said, stroking the animal's flank.

'Not a hope in hell,' Sam said.

'Pity, sure would like to own him.'

'Well this is as close as we're gonna get,' Sam said.

'Heard you had some trouble here,' Will said nonchalantly.

Young Arnie was about to answer when Sam

butted in. 'Yeah, we heard that, too. Pays not to get involved when there's gunplay.'

'But Mr Sam—' Arnie began, but that was as far as he got.

'Get those empty stalls cleaned out, boy. I ain't tellin' you agen!'

Wordlessly, Arnie turned away and walked to the empty stalls.

'So you've no idea who was shot at?' Will asked carelessly. 'Or whether he was killed or not?'

'Nope. Like I said, pays to keep away from gunplay in Virginny City. Anything else I can do for you, mister?'

Will caught the look of the young boy's face as he raked the dirty straw. That boy knew something! Will was convinced of that. Maybe he'd try and catch him alone sometime. See what he can dig out of him.

'Nah,' Will replied, 'unless you can recommend a boarding-house nearby.'

'There's plenty o' them, and hotels, too,' Sam replied. 'All much of a muchness, mister. I bunk down here so I ain't never stayed in none of 'em, so take your pick, I guess.'

'Thanks,' Will said, and you couldn't miss the sarcastic tone of his voice.

'Pleasure to be of service,' Sam answered, equally sarcastic.

Will decided to try the hotel across the street,

unbeknown to him, the same hotel that Sharper had booked into.

'Got a room?' Will asked.

'Sure have,' the desk clerk replied. 'How many nights?'

'Maybe two,' Will replied. 'I want a room that overlooks the main street.'

'No problem, sir. That's six dollars a night for a front room, so twelve in all.'

Will slammed down the money on the counter and was handed the key to room three.

He signed the register and took a note of the other names already there.

There were just two names who'd booked in over the last three days: Herbert Crookshank and Lem Walters. Rooms eleven and twelve.

Neither of the names meant a thing to him. Pushing the register back, he picked up his saddle-bag and rifle and headed for the stairs. At the top, he stopped and looked down the hallway to the side and rear of the hotel. He took a few steps down the hall and noted rooms eleven and twelve. The clerk, who had been watching, was about to call out directions, when Will turned and walked to his own room.

Unlocking the door he entered and threw his gear on to the bed. Crossing to the window, he pulled back the drapes and scanned the street, bustling with traffic as always. He had a good view of the comings and goings at the livery.

Will decided he couldn't stay in the room all the time on the off chance the man with the Arab came along. He needed information, and fast. Asking the sheriff was out of the question, but maybe he would try in the saloon. There was always gossip to be had in a saloon. Besides, he needed to get the dust out of his throat. He poured some water into a bowl and splashed his face, then slicked down his hair. Ready to leave, he donned the borrowed Stetson, left the room and, taking a look down the hallway, descended the stairs.

There was no one at the desk, so he pocketed his key and left the hotel. Stepping on to Main Street he could feel the heat rising from the ground and that made him even thirstier. The America Saloon was next door to the livery, separated only by the alleyway that led around the back. It was mid-afternoon and the saloon was buzzing. Not with miners – too early in the day for them – but mainly city folk in dandy suits, smoking expensive cigars and drinking imported whisky.

Apart from him, there were three mean-looking *hombres* sitting at a table near the bar in the far corner of the saloon. Will's brief glance around the room seemed to linger on the three men, who stared back at him with none-too-friendly eyes.

'What'll it be, mister,' a surly barkeep asked Will.

'Beer.'

A foam-filled glass was placed in front of him. 'Fifty cents,' the 'keep said, holding his hand out.

Will handed over a dollar. 'Another,' he said.

Will poured the beer down his parched throat and had finished the glass before the second one arrived. The beer was warm and not as refreshing as Will had expected, but nevertheless, it quenched his thirst. Taking out his makings, Will started to roll a cigarette when he noticed people beginning to edge away from him. Some of the fat businessmen were leaving the saloon, trying not to be noticed and the general din of the saloon was much quieter.

Will checked the mirror behind the bar. It wasn't his imagination; the saloon was emptying fast and the three men still sitting in the corner of the bar were now eyeing him with a malicious stare. The 'keep was down the far end of the bar, making a big fuss of the bar top with a cloth. Will lit his cigarette, not taking his eyes from the mirror. The atmosphere was thick with tension, which Will didn't understand, but something was sure going down.

Keeping his cool and his wits about him, Will casually finished his beer, stomped out his ciga- rette and turned to leave the saloon. He had no wish to be caught up in something that didn't concern him, so he'd try another saloon to see if he could discover the fate of the man he had shot.

'Goin' somewhere, mister?' a voice rapped out.

Will stopped in his tracks, his right hand moved instinctively to his gun butt.

'I'm talking to you, mister!' the same voice again.

Will turned round slowly.

'Seems he might be a mite deaf,' another man said.

'What's it to you, mister?' Will said.

'He don't recognize us, boys.'

'You got me confused with someone else,' Will said, and turned to leave.

'Oh, we ain't confused, mister, an' you ain't goin' nowheres till we get our money back.'

'What money?' Will asked, but already the faces of the three men were becoming familiar.

'You sold us a bum claim, an' to my way o' thinkin' you owe us.' The man took a step forward and was joined by his two *compadres*.

'No guarantees in this world, mister,' Will replied.

'You didn't own the stake! Now it's either our money or your hide!'

Will decided he had two options: lie and tell them he'd get their money, or draw, hoping they weren't gunnies and take them by surprise.

He made a bad choice.

Will's Colt cleared leather, but he squeezed the trigger too early and his shot was low, hitting one of the men in the foot. The other two blasted into him and he shot back like a rag doll. One slug caught him in the chest, the other in the lower jaw. He was dead before he hit the sawdust-covered floor. A pool of blood was spreading across the floor as the men re-holstered.

'Dang fool thought he could outdraw three of us. He drew first, you all saw that?'

The few men who had remained curious enough to find out what was going on, murmured their agreement. The barkeep, who had ducked behind the counter with just his head showing was quick to agree.

'Saw it all. He drew first all right.'

Sheriff Prady was on the scene within minutes. Scattergun in hand, he pushed through the batwings to see the body of an almost decapitated man lying in a pool of his own blood. Looking up he saw another man lying on the floor with a bloody boot.

'What the hell's going on in here?' he demanded.

'Man drew on us, Sheriff. We shot in self-defence,' the leader of the trio answered.

Prady turned to the barkeep. 'That so, Vince?'

'Sure was, Sheriff. The guy drew first, shot yonder man in the foot before the other two drew.'

'Anyone know who this is – was?' the sheriff asked.

'Critter sold us a staked claim on the foothills yonder, Sheriff. Turns out the deeds were fake. He didn't even own the piece o' the land. We jus' wanted our money back.'

'Know his name?' the sheriff asked.

'Nope. He was one o' four fellas who claimed they was sellin' up and heading north to 'Frisco,' the man answered. 'No names were mentioned and we didn't ask for any.'

'You must be loco to buy a stake like that,' the sheriff commented.

'We bought it through a lawyer,' came the retort, 'so we thought everything was legal and above board.'

'An' who was this lawyer?'

There was silence for a moment; the three looked sheepish.

'Guess you don't have his name either,' the sheriff said. 'You got the deeds?'

'The deeds were being prepared for us.'

'So you got no names and no deeds,' the sheriff said, shaking his head.

'Maybe it weren't the smartest move we ever made,' the man replied.

'Can someone get a doc?' the man on the floor asked. 'Sure is painful down here.'

'Someone go fetch a doc,' the sheriff said. 'You better get the undertaker, too.'

Sam was standing just outside the batwings and

he beckoned to the sheriff.

'What is it, Sam?'

'That there fella was in the livery earlier, asking a lotta questions.'

'Questions about what?' the sheriff asked.

'The shootin', o' course,' Sam replied.

'What sorta questions?' Prady asked.

'Wanted to know if the fella had been killed or not.'

'What did you tell him?'

'Nothin'. Told him I didn't see a thing,' Sam replied.

At that moment the doc arrived and started to attend to the wounded man, who was still lying on the floor.

'Hmmm. You got two choices, mister,' the doc said. 'I can pull your boot off, which will be painful, or I can cut it off. Your choice.'

'Hell I don't wanna lose a boot! Pull it off, Doc!'

The doc bent down and got a bite-bar out of his bag and told the man to clench it between his teeth. Then, taking hold of the boot heel in both hands, he pulled. The man let out a grunted yell through his clenched teeth as the boot, after two or three strong pulls, came off.

'Well,' the doc said, 'you were lucky. Just shot your little toe off.'

'You call that lucky?' the man resounded.

'Coulda been worse,' the doc grinned. 'You

coulda lost your foot.' The bleeding had almost stopped and it didn't take the doc long to bind the foot up.

'Come and see me in two days so I can change the dressing,' he said. 'That'll be ten dollars.'

'Ten dollars!'

'You want to get infected and lose your foot, maybe your leg, too?'

The man grunted and fished in his pocket.

'I got seven dollars, Doc. That's all the money I got left.'

'OK, I guess seven'll do.' The doc took the money. 'Don't forget, see me in two days' time.'

'Thanks, Doc.'

The undertaker was not so sympathetic.

'Who the hell's paying for his funeral?' he rasped.

'Check his pockets,' one of the men answered. 'He's had enough of our money.'

Doc James went through the man's pockets and came up with fifty dollars. 'Well, I'll take three of that,' he said, 'to make up my fee.'

He handed the rest to the sheriff.

'OK, Barney,' the sheriff said to the undertaker, 'send me the bill. Seems this critter can pay for his own funeral.'

Sharper was getting restless. Being cooped up was not his idea of pleasure, so when Sam came into

51

the barbershop to tell of the shooting, and the fact that the dead man had been asking questions, Sharper was immediately interested.

'Reckon I'll go take a looksee at this fella,' he said. 'Might be one of the men who slugged me.'

'He's over at Barney's, the undertaker. I'd hurry if'n I was you; ol' Barney don't hang around.'

Sharper donned his Stetson, hitched up his gun-belt and asked directions for the undertaker's place. Then he left the barbershop and made his way along Main, past the saloon and down to the next block.

The undertaker's place was a sombre-looking building, the façade painted black, with a one-word sign painted in white: UNDERTAKER'S. Sharper knocked on the front door and heard a gruff voice call out: 'It ain't locked!'

Entering the gloomy interior, Sharper saw a weedy little man behind a desk. His long black hair was tied back in a ponytail. His features were sharp; a long pointed nose separated two eyes that were like slits. His bony fingers were sorting through papers on the desk and without looking up the man said, 'Yes?'

'You have a fella in here I wanna see,' Sharper said.

'I got a few fellas in here, mister,' came the offhand reply.

'Fella was killed in the saloon, no more'n an

hour ago,' Sharper said.

'And how is that your business?'

Sharper's hand moved to the butt of his Smith & Wesson.

'Mister, I ain't got the time or the inclination for conversation. Where's the body?'

The scrawny little man stood. Sharper almost grinned, as the man was hardly any taller than when he was sitting.

'Ain't much to see; most of his face has been shot away.'

'Lead the way, mister,' Sharper said, and the little man opened a door at the rear of the office space and went through.

The room they entered was piled high with coffins.

'Business must be brisk,' Sharper commented.

'Can't complain,' the man said, turning, he held his hand out, 'Barney Gilpin,' he said.

Sharper gripped the hand, feeling nothing but dry bone. 'Sharper,' he replied.

Pushing through another door revealed a row of waist-high tables, three of which had a shroud-covered body on them. One body, naked, was being worked on by an even smaller man with hair whiter than snow.

'That's him,' Barney pointed at the body. 'Ain't much to see of his face, 'cept from the nose up. Slug took his chin clean off.'

53

Sharper stared at the face, not recognizing him at all. 'He have any papers on him?' he asked.

'Nah, not a thing. Had some money, which the sheriff has. Had the clothes he stood in and his handgun and Bowie, nothing else.' Barney lifted up one of the dead man's arms. It was stiff.

'Gonna plant him within the hour,' added the undertaker. 'Don't pay to keep 'em in here too long. The smell, see.'

As they left the room, the white-haired old man began to sew the shroud round the body.

'So, he a friend o' yours?' Barney asked.

'Nope. Ain't never seen him afore. You said you had his gun rig here?'

'Sure have,' Barney said, and walked across the coffin room to his front office. There, hanging on the wall was a shabby-looking rig. Barney took it off the hook and handed it to Sharper. 'Nothing on it to say who owns it,' he said.

Sharper didn't say anything as he first inspected the gun-belt, then took out the Colt. An old Navy Colt, well used by the look of it, but well maintained. He checked the butt of the weapon. Rubbing his thumb over the gun butt, Sharper inspected the small red smear left on his thumb.

It was blood.

And Sharper was pretty sure it was his blood.

'We better get goin',' Bart Sampson said. 'Be

nightfall soon an' I wanna get that claim further up the hillside.'

'Ain't we gonna wait for Will?' Ben asked.

'Nah. There's no guarantee he'll be back tonight. I reckon he'll stay over. Could take a while for him to find out any info.'

'We can handle two old-timers, anyways,' Clem put in. 'Soon as we lay claim to that site the sooner we can sell it on.'

'OK, check your weapons and let's ride,' Bart said.

It was late afternoon as the three men set off. The sky was a hazy blue and the sun's rays were still bright, casting long, inky-black shadows on the ground. They rode up the hillside. All around them they could hear the chink of metal on rock as prospectors dug into the ground hoping to find that illusive mother lode. The stream that meandered down the hillside was the site of a hive of activity. Men with great metal pans were sifting through the ground-up rocks, ever hopeful of finding gold. The stake they were aiming for was set higher up the hillside, quite isolated from the other claims, and was situated near the head of the stream. No one took any notice of the three riders as they wound their way up the hillside, each man there too intent on finding their fortunes.

Bart raised his hand and the trio stopped. 'There it is,' he said pointing up towards a squared-off partition of land. There were two men there but all that could be seen was their pickaxes as they rose and fell in the hole they'd dug. Dismounting, the three men ground-hitched their animals and climbed the few yards to the claim. Bart put his finger to his lips and said, in a hushed voice, 'Remember, no gunplay. Got that?'

'Bart,' Clem said, 'you say that every time and every time there ain't never no gunplay.'

Bart ignored this and motioned for them to enter the claim.

The digging hadn't missed a beat. The two old prospectors were too engrossed to notice anything.

'Howdy, boys,' Bart said to the two men.

Instantly they stopped digging and looked up at the figure looming over their hole. Although they didn't show it, both prospectors were more than a little alarmed. Two more figures stood over the hole, seeming like giants.

'What can we do for you, fellas?' One of the prospectors said.

'Well, it's simple, really,' Bart started, 'You see, this here is now our claim.'

'Like hell it is!' came the instant reply.

Bart didn't reply straight away. Instead, he took out his hunting knife and slowly ran his thumb along its razor-sharp edge.

'Sorry? Don't think I heard what you said,' Bart

smiled, a sickly, sneering grin.

'I said,' one of the old-timers started, 'like hell it is!'

Bart knelt down, bringing his face within a foot of the speaker and stared into the man's eyes. 'Mister, you got but two choices here: leave or die!'

In a slow laboured movement, one of the gold-diggers went for his gun, which was hitched in his pants top. The barrel snagged on his clothing as he tried to get it out. It was too late. In a flash, Ben Doyle had thrown his knife; the ten-inch blade penetrated the old man's chest with such force it was buried up to the hilt.

For a few moments there was absolute silence. The old man was still standing, his right hand holding the butt of his sidearm. But he was already dead.

He just hadn't realized it yet.

His legs began to buckle and slowly, he slid to the ground without making a sound. His partner just stood and stared. The speed at which it had happened hadn't registered with the old man and he was incapable of any movement or sound.

'Now what you say I give you a hand up, old-timer?' Bart said.

Still gripping his pickaxe, the old man stood his ground. He knew he had no chance with these three fellas. He also knew they'd kill him anyway, whatever he did. Almost imperceptibly, the old man brought his pickaxe arcing through the air, its sharp end piercing the right boot of Bart.

Try as he might, Bart couldn't contain the agonized scream that filled his throat. The sound seemed to bounce off the rocks, echoing and echoing until it died out. Without hesitation, Clem threw his knife. As accurately as Ben's, the knife buried itself in the old man's chest. Bart, meanwhile, was down on one knee. His right foot was pinned to the ground, and as the old man fell to the floor to join his partner, the weight of the pickaxe, no longer being supported, eased itself out of Bart's foot, and clattered to the ground, leaving Bart in even greater pain.

'You OK, Bart?' Clem asked.

'What sort of a dumb-ass question is that?' Bart almost shrieked. 'I just got my foot pinned to the ground with a pickaxe and you ask if I'm OK? Well I ain't OK. OK?'

'No need to mouth off at me, I was only askin',' Clem said.

'Get over here and help me get this damn boot off.'

As Clem moved across to help Bart, Ben jumped into the hole and retrieved both knives; having wiped the blood off them on the dead men's clothing, he put them in his belt.

'Goddamn, you were lucky.' Clem said as he stared at Bart's foot. 'Damn pickaxe went right between your toes. You jus' got two little cuts.'

'Well, they hurt like all hell,' Bart whined.

'Ain't bleedin' any, figure you can ride?' Clem asked.

'Yeah, sure I can ride.'

'Well we'll tidy up here and get back to the shack. We'll be along as soon as we can an' I'll fix your foot up good and proper.'

'OK, you get them bodies over to the ridge and dump 'em with the rest,' Bart ordered, somewhat ashamed now about the howling he'd done and needing to assert his authority once again.

'Sure, sure,' Clem said.

Bart hobbled over to his horse and mounted up, silently, even though his foot was beginning to throb.

Clem called down to Ben, 'OK, let's get these stiffs outa there,' he said.

With a great deal of effort, Ben handed up the bodies of the two old men and Clem laid them on the ground. He went through their pockets, but found nothing of value. Ben joined him and they belly-laid the two men across their horses and mounted up.

The ridge they were heading for was only around a hundred yards away and they easily climbed the steep gradient to reach it. Dismounting, they peered over the almost perpendicular drop of some thousand feet into the chasm below.

'Let's get this done,' Ben said.

They hauled off the bodies and watched as they fell like rag dolls, bounding off the rock face, arms and legs waving uncontrollably. There was a dull thud, followed by another, as the dead men hit the bottom.

'That's them done for,' Clem said.

'Let's get back to the site and go through their stuff.

The prospector's gear didn't amount to much – they never expected it to be a great haul – however, the small amount of gold dust in a leather pouch was an added bonus.

But they found what they were looking for: the deeds.

The pair of eyes watching them never faltered. He hadn't seen the killings, but he saw the two dead bodies being hauled away and now watched as the old-timers' gear was ransacked. Got you at last, he mouthed to himself.

CHAPTER 5

Sharper left the undertaker's. His next visit was to the three men involved in the shooting. He found them back in the saloon.

'How's the foot?' Sharper asked the man with his leg perched on a chair.

'Mister, it's as sore as all hell in a bucket,' the man answered.

Sharper grinned.

'Mind if I join you, fellas?' Sharper asked.

'Man can do a lot o' joinin' with a drink,' one of the men answered.

'Fair point,' Sharper agreed. He gestured to the 'keep who waddled across the floor, glasses clutched in his hands.

'Bring a bottle,' Sharper said, 'and not that rat's piss you serve up. The good stuff.'

'That'll be five dollars,' the 'keep replied. 'Up front.'

Sharper gave him a withering look before reaching into his vest pocket. He withdrew some folding money and handed over the five dollars. 'It'd better be worth it,' he said before releasing the note.

'Mister, if'n you don't think it tastes like nectar from the gods of whiskey, you can have your money back.'

Sharper nodded and released the five-dollar note.

The 'keep returned immediately and placed a full bottle and an extra glass on the table. 'Enjoy, gents,' he said and walked away.

Sharper picked up the bottle, pulled the cork out with his teeth and spat it on the floor and poured four shots. 'Your health, gentlemen,' he said and drained his glass.

'Didn't get a name, mister,' one of the men said.

'Wade, Sharper Wade. Folks just call me Sharper.'

'I'm Mick O'Hara, this here's Des Malone and tenderfoot yonder,' he paused to laugh at his own joke, 'is Abe Montana.'

'Good to meet you, fellas,' Sharper said, then: 'I'm mighty interested in that fella you shot.'

'Was self-defence, mister,' Mick shot out.

'I ain't the law,' Sharper added quickly, and related the story of the killing of Soo Lee and her grandfather. 'So you see, I got a vested interest in this fella.' Sharper paused, looking at each man in turn. 'I saw three of the men who shot the girl and the old man, but the fourth man, the man who slugged me, I believe is the fella you shot. You get a look at his partners?' Sharper asked.

'Sure did, that's why we park ourselves in here all day. We're waitin' on them to come in, and when they do—'

'When they do,' Sharper cut in, 'you come tell me or the sheriff. You tryin' to kill them ain't gonna get you your money back. I aim to bring them to justice, not have a shootin' party.'

'That's a tall order, mister; my trigger finger sure does get itchy when I think o' them critters and my money.' Mick fell silent.

'You got a choice: a possible hangin' or some if not all, of your money back,' Sharper reasoned.

'OK, makes sense, I guess. We'll go along with you, but I gotta warn you, anything happens to you, or you don't catch 'em, we go a-gunnin' after them.'

'Fair enough,' Sharper said. 'I'm stayin' with Harvey, the barber across the way, you hear or see anything, come find me. And one final thing,' Sharper paused, not sure how to word what he was going to say next.

'No matter what you hear or read about me, ignore it.' He stood and began to walk away.

'Mister,' Mick called after him, 'you left your whiskey.'

'Have it on me,' Sharper said and left the saloon.

'What the hell did he mean by that?' Des Malone said.

'Danged if I know, but I guess in the fullness of time—'

'I need to speak to Mr Clemens,' Sharper told the desk clerk.

'Mr Clemens? Oh, you mean Mr Twain. May I ask what it's about, sir?'

'It's kinda personal, but a story that will interest Mr Cl— Twain,' Sharper said.

'And your name, sir?'

'Sharper Wade.'

'Take a seat, Mr Wade, I'll see if Mr Twain is free.'

Five minutes later a dapper man with a huge bushy moustache stood before Sharper.

'Mr Wade?'

'Yes, Mr Twain?'

'How can I help you, Mr Wade? I only have five minutes to spare, I'm afraid. Deadline is looming.'

'Anywhere we can talk – in private?' Sharper asked.

'Certainly, come through to my office,' Twain answered, and led the way through a maze of desks to the far side of the building.

'Now, what's your story?' Twain asked.

Sharper related his tale in great detail, leaving

nothing out. 'So you see,' he concluded, 'I reckon the body over at the undertaker's is the fella who slugged me, and I also reckon he was sent to town to kill me.'

'But how can I help?' Twain asked.

'Easy; you can report my death,' Sharper replied.

'And how will that help?'

'Well, I figure the other three are lying low cos they know I can finger 'em. If they think I'm dead they'll have no worries and might come out of their hideout.'

Mark Twain didn't reply straight away; he was pondering the possibilities. Printing flagrant lies with his name as the byline, was not something he did lightly.

Then he reached a decision.

'Under normal circumstances, Mr Wade, I would never entertain such a notion, but I can see your point of view. All right, I'll write the piece.' There was a short pause: 'But I must insist as few people as possible know of our deception.'

'There'll be just you, me, the sheriff and old Harvey,' Sharper replied.

Twain nodded and stood up, indicating the meeting was over.

'I appreciate that, Mr Twain, an' as soon as I catch those murdering bastards, you'll be the first to know about it.'

The two men shook hands and Sharper left the building.

'You get them deeds?' Bart asked as Clem and Ben returned to the disused line shack.

'Sure did, and we got rid of the bodies, too.' Clem handed over the title deeds to the claim.

'Nice work,' Bart said. 'You mind fixing up my foot?'

'Sure thing, Bart, let's take a looksee,' Ben said.

Ben knelt by Bart's foot. 'Ain't too bad – just a nick on two toes – but I better clean it up some. No tellin' where that pickaxe has been,' he said, laughing.

'Pass me the whiskey bottle, Clem,' Ben said.

Pulling the cork out Ben looked at Bart: 'This might sting a tad.'

Bart nearly hit the roof as Ben poured a liberal amount of rotgut on his foot. He grabbed the bottle and took a mighty swig. It didn't ease the pain any, but he felt better for it.

'I'll bind your foot, but you best keep off it for a day or two; don't want any infection there, pal,' Ben said. He retrieved the whiskey bottle and, taking a good mouthful, he passed it to Clem.

'Will should be back in the morning,' Bart said. 'Hope he's got some good news for us.'

'Either way, we gotta get these deeds to Lance, so's he can fix 'em up for us. Sooner we sell that claim the better,' Clem said.

'Well, we got ourselves some whiskey and vittals, so we'd better make the best of it tonight,' Bart said and reached for the whiskey bottle again.

Sheriff Prady listened intently as Sharper revealed his plan.

'OK,' the sheriff said at last, 'we need to make sure you ain't seen but can see. Is Harvey all right with you staying there? There's a good view of the main street from the upstairs window. Next, I have to make sure those three fellas believe you died from gunshot wounds, maybe blood poisoning.'

'Just keep it simple,' Sharper said. 'Ol' Harvey says I can stay as long as I like, so there's no problem there. Oh, and keep your deputy in the dark, OK?'

'Barney has already taken out the bodies he had to Boot Hill, so, mister, I guess you are dead!'

Sharper smiled. 'Now we wait,' he said.

By noon the next day, the trio of Ben, Clem and Bart were getting both annoyed and uneasy.

'Where the hell is Will?' Bart demanded, as if the other two would know.

'He shoulda been back by now, unless something's gone wrong,' Ben said.

'What the hell could've gone wrong?' Bart bellowed. 'All he had to do was find out if that critter was dead or not and if he was alive, then kill him!

67

What's so difficult about that?'

Neither Ben nor Clem replied. They knew what the hell could go wrong.

'We gotta get those deeds into the lawyer, pronto,' Bart went on.

'I'll take 'em in,' Clem said. 'See if I can find Will at the same time.'

'That's risky,' Ben said. 'What if you bump into this guy?'

'It's a big city, Ben, I think the chances of that are pretty remote.'

Bart considered their position before saying: 'We ain't got no choice. You'll have to go, Clem. Who knows, you might even meet Will on the way out here.'

Arnie arrived back at the livery stable at his normal time of two in the afternoon. His shift lasted until well after dark as Sam always had himself a siesta in the afternoon. Today was no different.

Sam saw Arnie come in but instead of his usual, bouncy self, Arnie was both withdrawn and pale. 'You feeling OK, Arnie?' Sam asked.

Arnie didn't reply for some time and Sam could see the boy was in some sort of turmoil. 'I seen something awful, Mr Sam,' Arnie eventually said.

'Spit it out, boy, what did you see?'

'I saw – I saw some killin',' Arnie managed to get out.

'Come on, boy, start at the beginning and tell me all about it,' Sam said and patted a straw bale for Arnie to come sit on.

'Well, you know I like to walk in the foothills most mornings,' Arnie began.

'Sure, still looking for that illusive nugget, eh?'

'Yeah. I'll find one, one day,' Arnie said and gave a small smile.

'So this killin'?' Sam prompted.

'Well, I was up near the north ridge, just kicking stones and stuff, when I hear these voices. I ducked down behind a thicket and could just make out three cowboys and they was jus' a-talkin' to a hole in the ground.

'Then one of the men took out a knife and threw it down the hole and then I see a pickaxe come up and hit one of the cowboys as another knife was thrown in the hole.' Arnie's voice was getting higher and higher.

'OK, son, calm down now. What happened next?'

'What happened next was sure sickenin',' Arnie said and was quiet for a spell.

'I watched them drag two old-timers outa that hole and drag them to the ridge. They just pushed 'em over, Mr Sam! Just pushed 'em over.'

'You recognize any of 'em?' Sam asked.

'No, sir, I ain't never seen 'em afore.'

'We better get over to the sheriff an' tell him all

69

about this,' Sam said. 'Come on, boy, let's shake a leg!'

Lance Whittaker was a lawyer by profession and a crook by choice. In his early thirties, he resembled a penguin. Short and fat with a large nose and small, slitty eyes he waddled rather than walked. His suit, bought back East, was flash as was his waistcoat, which bulged at the buttons as it tried vainly to keep his bulbous belly in. Initially he was a laughing stock until he killed a man in a shoot-out. It was a fair fight but no one expected the little fat man to be able to draw as fast as he did.

So it didn't take Lance Whittaker long to discover there was more money to be made illegally than by honest endeavour. Besides, he was the only lawyer who wore a gun so despite his physical demeanour, he attracted a lot of attention from the lower section of society. Whittaker hadn't had a single client since he arrived in Virginia City. He'd put himself about a bit, handing out flyers at every opportunity, but with no luck.

The claim-jumping scam had been his idea, and a money-spinner it was, too. The hardest part of the plan had been to find the right men, and there he had had been fortunate. Silas Marsh was one of twelve deputy sheriffs in Virginia City – and a disgruntled one. He was the most senior of deputies but drew the same meagre pay as everyone else. Whittaker was certain he could manipulate the man with promises of riches. But how to approach the man without getting arrested?

Then he had his first stroke of luck.

A man had been arrested for murder and he had one of Whittaker's flyers on him. So his first case was a murder trial. On the face of it, it was an open and shut case – so certain were the powers that be, that the scaffold was being checked over – but not to Lance Whittaker. A miner working the Comstock Lode had been backshot in an alley and robbed of a small leather pouch of gold dust. Silas Marsh had been patrolling the area and was on the scene almost straight away. He had seen the suspect kneeling over the body and taking the pouch. Lance decided to have a word with Silas, the only prosecution witness.

He knew the man often drank in the America Saloon after his shift ended, so he made his way there the night before the trial was due to start. Entering the saloon, Whittaker spotted the deputy propping up the far end of the bar and he made his way across the crowded room.

'Deputy Marsh, how good to see you,' Whittaker said. 'A refill?'

'Mighty good of you, Mr Whittaker. Whiskey.'

'Call me Lance, I prefer that,' Whittaker said.

The two men made idle chitchat for a few

minutes before Lance directed the conversation the way he wanted it to go. 'Must be a mighty fine job, being a deputy,' he began.

'Hell, no,' Silas replied. 'You're just treated like the town's dogsbody and paid damn little for it.'

'Oh,' Lance said, 'I rather thought that a place as rich as this—'

'The place ain't rich. Comstock and his cronies are, the shopkeeper's and saloon owners sure are, even some of the miners strike it lucky, but law enforcement? Don't make me laugh.'

'There must be a million ways of making money here,' Lance pushed.

'Well it sure ain't in the law,' Silas grunted.

Lance ordered more drink, this time telling the 'keep to leave the bottle. 'Seems to me making money here is either luck or illegal,' Lance said.

'You got that right,' Silas said. 'Claim-jumpin' and selling on makes the money up there on the foothills.'

'How do you mean?' Lance asked.

'Hell, there ain't no gold or silver up there, leastways, not that prospectors can get at. It's down too deep in quartz an' they don't have the right tools.' Silas finished his drink and helped himself to another one.

'Maybe we should try our hand at that,' Lance said quietly.

Silas was quiet for a few moments before he

nodded: 'Hell, yes. Why not? We could make a bundle.'

'Keep your voice down, Silas,' Lance said, 'don't want to advertise it, do we.'

Silas put a finger over his lips in an exaggerated manner and Lance knew the man was putty in his hands.

'All we need do is find the right men for the job,' Lance said. 'I don't suppose you know of any offhand, do you?'

'I can think of one or two,' Silas answered.

'What about the man on trial tomorrow?' Lance asked.

'Hell, he'll be the centre of a necktie party, soon as the trial's over.'

'Did you actually see him shoot that miner?' Lance asked.

'Well, not exactly, but it was plain obvious he had.'

'How so?'

'Well, he was going through the dead man's pockets,' Silas said.

'Mr Sampson says he was looking to see if the man had any identification. Did you check his gun?' Lance asked.

'Er, well, no, not really,' Silas said.

'Not really? What does that mean? Either you did or you didn't.'

'I didn't.'

'I think we've found one of our men, Mr Marsh,'

Lance said as he downed a shot of whiskey.

'How do you mean?' Silas asked.

'You just answer those questions in the same way tomorrow in court. The prosecution has no witnesses. Get my drift?'

Silas was silent for a moment; he didn't get the drift at all. The whiskey was having an effect on him and his brain was closing down with every passing second. But still he answered, 'Yes.'

'We're going to be rich men, Mr Marsh. Very rich men.'

The court proceedings went exactly as Lance Whittaker wanted. The case was dismissed through lack of evidence. There was an audible groan from the assembled townsfolk as the judge spoke. Their hanging party had been spoiled.

'I'm free?'

'Yes, Mr Sampson, you're free – in a way,' Lance Whittaker replied.

'Either I'm free or I ain't,' Sampson said.

'Well, you ain't gonna hang, Mr Sampson, so in that respect you are free. But I have a little business proposal that could make you a wealthy man.' Lance Whittaker paused, waiting for a reaction.

'I'm listening, Mr Whittaker.'

Lance went on to explain his plan and how it would work. And so, Whittaker's claim-jumping scam was born.

*

'I can't sit around here all day doin' nothin',' Sharper said to Harvey.

'Well, you're dead, you cain't go out,' Harvey replied.

Then a sudden thought hit Harvey and his face lit up.

'Hell! A disguise!' he almost shouted. 'I can give you a disguise!' Harvey all but jumped up and down.

'How you gonna do that?' Sharper asked.

'In the past I done some costume work for travelling players, you know, wigs and beards and moustaches an' stuff from the hair I keep. I can make one for you, a beard or moustache, I mean,' Harvey said.

'Hell, that could work. Maybe a beard would be best,' Sharper said.

'OK,' Harvey replied, 'but you'll need another haircut, to keep the same colour.'

'Let's do it,' Sharper said, relieved that he could get out and track the killers down before he went stir crazy. He'd heard of cabin fever, and now he was beginning to feel like he was getting it.

It took Harvey nearly three hours to complete the beard. He fixed it to Sharper's face with spirit gum and then trimmed the side burns to match.

Sharper looked in the mirror. 'Hell, Harvey,

you're a real artist! Even I can't tell it's false,' he said, shaking Harvey by the hand.

'Well, at least I ain't lost it,' Harvey modestly replied.

Sharper donned his Stetson, checked his Colt and made his first port of call: the America Saloon.

'Howdy, stranger', the 'keep said. 'What can I get ya?'

It was the same bartender who'd served him before and he obviously didn't recognize him. Sharper let a small grin escape his lips before answering, 'Whiskey, and leave the bottle.'

'Coming right up, mister.'

Sharper turned and looked around the saloon. Most of the tables were occupied, mainly by miners who'd either finished their shift or were having a drink before they started. Sharper had heard Harvey say that temperatures reached 120 degrees Fahrenheit underground and the men worked wearing only shoes and breechclouts, and that around their feet, hot steamy water bubbled up from thermal springs. There were, of course, occasional deaths, either through accidents or by men drinking the poisoned water, despite being warned about it.

As Sharper surveyed the faces, one man stood out; a dapper dude who seemed out of place. Sitting at his table was a man Sharper recognized: Deputy Silas Marsh.

The 'keep placed a shot glass and a bottle on the counter. 'That'll be five bucks, mister,' he said, smiling.

Sharper reached into his vest pocket and pulled out some coins and handed them over. 'Say, who's the fat dapper guy with the deputy?' he asked, filling his glass.

'Him? That's Lance Whittaker, a lawyer. Got an office down yonder,' the 'keep pointed to his left, which meant little to Sharper.

Sharper thought no more about it until a third man arrived at the same table. He recognized this man, too. Sharper was about to approach the trio, when the new man and Whittaker stood up and left the saloon. Marsh stayed where he was for a few minutes, then he, too, made his way outside.

Sharper couldn't believe his luck in finding one of the murderers so quickly and he was determined not to lose him. 'Save the bottle for me,' he said to the 'keep and followed the deputy out into the street. He scanned the street and just caught sight of Whittaker and the man who had been a member of the gang who killed Soo Lee and her grandfather entering a building opposite. He paused on the boardwalk and lit a cigarette, watching the deputy.

Although trying to be inconspicuous, to Sharper's eyes, the deputy was continually scanning the street in both directions and, when he felt sure he wasn't being watched, he sidled up to the same building Whittaker had entered. Stopping again to scan the street, Silas knocked once and the door opened. The deputy disappeared inside.

Lance Whittaker sat behind his large mahogany desk and looked over the title deeds that Clem Watson had brought to him. 'Excellent work, Mr Watson,' Whittaker said. 'These halfwits still signing with an "X" makes life a lot easier.'

Both men tensed as they heard the knock on the door. Watson drew his six-gun as Whittaker went to make sure it was Marsh. Letting the man in, Whittaker went back to his desk and studied the deeds once more.

'We got a problem,' Silas began.

Both men looked at Silas.

'You were seen up in the foothills,' he stated.

'So?' Watson responded.

'You were seen dumping the bodies.'

'What! Who by?' Watson asked.

'That young kid Sam employs. Seems he roams the foothills in his spare time, on the lookout for gold.' Silas looked to both men. 'What are we gonna do?

'Who's Sam?' Watson asked.

'He runs the livery; young Arnie is his groom and general dogsbody,' Whittaker said.

'Then I better pay them a visit,' Watson said.

'You must take care of them,' Whittaker said.

'They could ruin the whole operation.'

'Don't worry, I will.' Watson stood and motioned for Silas to leave the office ahead of him.

'One more thing,' Silas said as he reached the door. 'Will done got hisself killed yesterday. Seems he bumped into some men you'd sold a claim site to. They buried him on Boot Hill this morning along with that stranger you slugged the other day.'

'He's dead too?' Clem couldn't believe his luck.

'Yep, Doc says he had a brain bleed and it killed him in his sleep.'

There was a stunned silence from both Clem and Lance as they absorbed the news.

'We gotta be more careful,' Lance said.

Silas grunted and left the office.

What the hell was going on there? Sharper wondered. His initial reaction was to confront the man, but what good would that do? He wanted the others, too. At least he had a link, of sorts: both Whittaker and Marsh knew who the man was. Sharper decided to question Harvey and see what he knew; he might even call upon Sam at the livery, too. Between them, those two old-timers seemed to know what gossip there was. Later, he thought, he'd have a quiet word with Sheriff Prady.

Sharper finished his cigarette and was about to move off to visit Harvey, when Marsh left the office.

Two minutes later, the newcomer left, but there was no sign of the lawyer. Marsh had turned left and the newcomer right. They were acting as if they didn't even know each other. Sharper watched as the two men strode away. Five minutes later, the lawyer left his office, locking the door behind him.

Sharper was in two minds: follow the killer or break into the office? He decided that at this juncture, neither would be appropriate. Whatever was going on didn't seem legal and Sharper was determined to get to the bottom of it – one way or the other.

CHAPTER 6

Clem Watson was pleased with the outcome his day's work in Virginia City. He had a description of the boy who'd seen them at the claim site, and the old man who ran the livery. All he had to do was kill them. And if there was one thing Clem was good at, it was killing.

Untying the reins from the hitch-rail, Clem walked his horse to the livery stable. Taking the side alley entrance, he hitched the horse outside. The alleyway was quiet, as he hoped it would be. At this time of the day, most folks who weren't down the mines were now at home awaiting supper. Keeping close to the plank wall, Watson chanced a look into the stables. It took a few moments for his eyes to get used to the gloom inside the livery, but then he saw some movement.

Clem reached behind his back and drew out his eight-inch throwing knife, so sharp it could split hairs. He waited till he had a clear sight of the man inside. In one fluid movement, Clem took aim and threw the knife. It hit the liveryman squarely in the back. Sam Russell never knew what hit him. Without a sound, Sam fell to the straw-covered floor. He survived for only a few minutes more, gasping for air as blood oozed from his back, pooling on the ground as his life ebbed away.

Clem calmly walked into the livery and, putting a foot on Sam's back, retrieved his knife. He wiped the blade on Sam's shirt and went to look for the boy.

Arnie had no idea what was going on. He was toting bales of hay from a wagon parked at the rear of the livery, and stacking them in the far corner.

His senses were alerted, however, as the animals, scenting blood, began to get restless. Arnie dropped a bale of hay and went to the nearest horse, stroking the animal's neck and uttering soothing sounds, thinking that he was the cause of their unrest. As he soothed the animal, his eyes locked on the man now facing him. A man Arnie recognized.

'You been talking too much, kid,' Clem said as he moved closer.

Arnie had nowhere to run. He was in a stall and there was no way out. His eyes were drawn like a magnet to the blade held in Clem's right hand. He stared at it, couldn't take his eyes of it; he was mesmerized. Backing further into the stall, the boy felt the wooden wall against his back.

Without another word, Clem, in an underarm action, threw his knife for a second time. As if in slow motion, Arnie watched as the blade flew through the air and thudded into his stomach. Traumatized, the boy never made a sound. The shock of the knife entering his body, and the red stain that seemed to instantly show through his thin cotton shirt, sent him into shock. He felt no pain as he slid to the floor.

Clem smiled. He walked past the agitated horse in the stall and knelt down to retrieve his knife, wiping the blade clean on the boy's pants leg. He stood, re-sheathed the knife and left the livery.

In all, it had taken him no more than three minutes to end the lives of two people. Once outside, he mounted up and set off back to his partners with the good news.

Sharper entered the barbershop as Harvey was sweeping the floor of hair – a seemingly endless task.

'Sharper,' Harvey greeted.

'Got some questions,' Sharper said, closing the door, locking it and turning the 'Open' sign round to 'Closed'.

'Sure thing,' Harvey said, 'let's get some coffee upstairs.

83

The two men climbed the stairs at the back of the shop and entered the front room that overlooked Main Street. Harvey poured two mugs of coffee, sat down opposite Sharper and waited. Sharper sipped at the hot brew for a few moments before saying, 'I saw one of the men in the saloon.'

'Hot diggedy!' Harvey said. 'You get him?'

'Well, I was about to, but he was sitting with someone else. A fat little dude called Lance Whittaker.'

'Whittaker! That crooked lawyer?'

'Not only that, they were joined by Silas Marsh,' Sharper added.

'Silas?'

'Yep. Then they all went to Whittaker's office. Tell me, Harvey, what's the news on Whittaker?'

'Well, mainly jus' rumours, but you know there's never smoke without fire. Seems there's bin a lot of shady claim-stakin' going on. Nothin' that can be proved, but Whittaker seems to be at the centre of it.'

'Shady claims in what way?' Sharper asked.

'Well, as I said, it's only rumours, but it seems prospectors have disappeared. Oh, it always seems to be above board; title deeds have been produced, but you know most of the fellas that work the small claims cain't read nor write, an' one "X" looks pretty much like another.'

'So what's the scam?' Sharper asked.

'Oh, that's simple; was explained to me by a geo-something or other,' Harvey began.

'Geologist?' Sharper said.

'That's the fella. Well, I was cutting his hair an' we got to yakkin', like you do an' he tol' me that the gold and silver deposits hereabouts are buried way too deep for pickaxes to ever reach 'em. Seems they's buried in quartz and you need special equipment to even get close to any gold.'

'Surely these prospectors know that?' Sharper said.

'Sharper, you ever hear o' gold fever?'

'Sure.'

'Well, it mashes your brain up. All these folks need is to be shown a small nugget or some dust and they're in up to their armpits.'

'So they buy these claims thinking they're gonna strike it rich, huh?' Sharper said, stroking his false beard. After a brief pause, he asked, 'What about Silas? What's his role in all this?'

'Ya got me beat there,' Harvey said. 'I've known Silas for years, as has ol' Sam, an' I always thought him a decent, honest, upright person.'

'Hmm,' Sharper mused. 'Well seems to me he's involved in all this. Think I'll go see Sam, see what he has to add.'

'Well, I'll have some vittals ready for when you get back,' Harvey said. 'Chicken OK?'

'Chicken's fine,' Sharper said. He finished his

coffee and got up to leave.

'How's that beard holdin' up?' Harvey asked.

'Just fine,' Sharper said. 'Gettin' kinda used to it.'

'I tell ya, they're both dead. Buried this morning,' Clem said.

'Seems like our luck's riding,' Bart said.

'I doubt Will would agree with you,' Ben said.

'Well at least there are no witnesses left,' Clem said.

'Ain't you forgettin' somethin'?' Ben said.

'Like what?' Bart asked.

'Those cowboys we sold that claim to, they recognized Will, so chances are, they'd recognize us, too.'

'Goddamn!' Bart said eventually. 'We better sort them fellas out as well.'

'We?' Clem said. 'You ain't in no fit state to sort anything out with that foot o' yourn.'

'I can sit a horse as good as any man,' Bart retorted.

'Maybe so,' Ben said, 'but we cain't jus' go in shootin', we gotta bushwhack them fellas. If'n we don't kill 'em, we might as well pack up and move on.'

'Yeah,' Clem added. 'We gotta be careful. Me'n Ben will sort this out.'

'Well you best do it soon. I don't want them

showing up at the door with guns blazing,' Bart said.

'I gotta eat and get some shuteye first,' Clem said. 'We'll ride into town as it gets dark and bide our time. I 'member those three, all right. I can feel my knife itching for action already.' Clem smiled, a sickly smile that sent shivers down Bart's spine.

'Sam? Sam, you in here?' Sharper called out.

There was no reply.

'Arnie, you about?'

Again only silence greeted his call. Sharper was puzzled. Sam never left the livery unattended. It was then he spotted the body. He knelt by Sam's side and felt for a pulse he already knew wasn't there. 'Goddamn!' he muttered.

Then his thoughts went to the boy, Arnie. He quickly searched through the stables until he suddenly stopped, listening intently. Above the sound of the animals' snickering and the occasional hoof beating at the straw-covered floor, he thought he heard a groan. Straining his ears as hard as he could, Sharper heard the sound again.

'Arnie? Is that you?'

There was no reply. So he headed for the stalls, searching each one until he came across the crumpled body of the boy.

'Jeez!' Sharper muttered as he knelt down. The

boy's eyes flickered open briefly. 'Stay calm, Arnie. I'll go fetch the doc. You're gonna be OK,' Sharper said. Then he looked at the boy's stomach, his shirt stained a dark red. 'Just keep still; the doc'll be right over. I won't be long.'

'Hold it right there, mister. One false move and you're a dead man!'

Sharper turned to see Silas Marsh, gun drawn and pointed at Sharper's chest.

'What the hell!' Sharper turned to face the voice. 'Silas, get a doc, quick.'

'I ain't goin' anywhere,' Silas replied. 'You're under arrest for murder!'

'Are you crazy? This boy's still alive,' Sharper said.

'Not for much longer,' Silas said, between gritted teeth.

Sharper slowly stood.

'I'm warnin' you, no sudden moves,' Silas said.

'Silas?' The barber had arrived at the livery barn.

'Stay outa this, Harvey, I got me a killer here,' Silas said.

'You dang fool, don't you know who this is?' Harvey said, then looked at Sharper, who had a finger over his lips to indicate silence, Harvey stopped talking.

'Go fetch the doc, Harvey,' Sharper said. 'Arnie's still alive.'

Sharper saw the look on Silas's face. He was undecided on what to do.

'OK, go fetch him, Harvey. You, we're heading to the jail.' Silas pulled the hammer back on his Colt and motioned for Sharper to move. Reaching forward, Silas removed Sharper's side iron and prodded him in the back. 'Git moving!'

Doc James knelt by Arnie's side and inspected the wound. 'You better get back to my surgery, Harvey. Fetch the stretcher and grab a couple of fellas. I'll need to operate, an' quickly.'

'He gonna be OK, Doc?' Harvey asked.

'Too early to tell, but it's bad,' the doc replied.

Harvey was back within five minutes with two men and the stretcher.

'Get this horse into another stall,' the doc said, 'then we'll have to very carefully get Arnie on to the stretcher.'

One of the men led the animal to an empty stall, then the four men gently lifted a groaning Arnie as best they could.

'Thanks, boys,' the doc said, 'you can leave now.' The doc got to work. With the aid of his nurse, he cut Arnie's shirt off and cleaned up the small entry wound. Arnie was semi-conscious, so he applied a chloroform-soaked cloth to the boy's mouth and waited till the youngster slipped into unconsciousness.

Then Doc James began to inspect the internal damage.

'What's the charge?' Sheriff Prady asked as Silas pushed Sharper roughly through the door.

'Murder!' Silas replied, 'He done killed ol' Sam and tried to kill Arnie. Caught him red-handed.' Silas roughly pushed Sharper into an empty cell and locked the door. 'I'll get back to the livery and see to Sam,' the deputy said.

'OK. Check out Arnie too,' Prady said.

'Yeah, sure, I'll check out Arnie,' Silas replied and left the sheriff's office.

By the time Silas returned to the livery, Arnie had been taken away and the undertaker was in the process of wrapping Sam's body in a cotton shroud, ready to go to the morgue.

'How's the boy?' Silas asked.

'Doc's taken him – don't look good, though,' the undertaker answered.

Silas thought he'd better take a visit to Lance Whittaker. Things hadn't gone exactly to plan. If Arnie recovered and told his story, then not only was the whole operation at risk, but Silas's involvement would be obvious.

The boy had to be silenced.

CHAPTER 7

'Sheriff,' Sharper called out. There was no immediate reply, so Sharper called again.

From the front office a voice replied, 'I'm busy! I'll come through when I'm good and ready.'

'It's me, Sharper Wade.'

That brought an immediate reaction. The sheriff came through the door to the cells.

'Sharper?'

'Yeah, it's me. Harvey made this beard for me.'

'Well I'll be a—' The sheriff scratched his head. 'Sure didn't recognize you.'

'That was the objective,' Sharper replied.

'What the hell's going on here?' the sheriff asked.

'Not sure yet,' Sharper said. 'But it involves Silas, that lawyer, Whittaker, and the four men who killed Soo Lee and her grandfather.'

'Silas? Nah, that can't be right. Silas is a good man.'

'That's as maybe,' Sharper replied. 'But I tell you, he's involved. I saw him and Whittaker in the saloon earlier. They were joined by one of the four men who did the killings.'

'Who killed Sam and Arnie, then?' Sheriff Prady asked.

'Well, not me, that's for sure. And Arnie ain't dead – yet! I sent Harvey for the doc, so I hope he's gonna survive.'

'But Silas said he caught you red-handed?'

'Not so sure that was a coincidence,' Sharper replied. 'I found Sam already dead – looked like a knife wound in his back. Arnie was still alive when I got there.'

Sheriff Prady went back to the front office and returned almost straight away with a large bunch of keys. He unlocked the door and let Sharper out. 'For a stranger in town you sure get into a lot of trouble,' he said, leading the way back to the office.

'Seems to follow me, Bill,' Sharper replied. 'I need to get to the doc's. Find out how Arnie is. It can't be a coincidence that they were attacked.'

'You figure they're involved in whatever it is too?' the sheriff asked.

'I doubt it,' Sharper replied. 'But they might have found something out.'

Prady took Sharper's gun-rig down from a hook. 'Well whatever which way, I ain't got no reason to hold you here.'

'I'll keep in touch,' Sharper said. 'After I've seen the doc, I'll try and find out what Silas is up to.'

'Not much I can do to help,' Bill Prady said wistfully. 'Try an' avoid any gunplay, I don't want the marshal poking his nose in, OK?'

'I'll do my best, Bill,' Sharper said with a wink.

Sharper headed for Doc James's place, but there was no news there as the doc was still operating. Promising to come back later, Sharper thought about his next move. Obviously, Silas Marsh had not recognized him, so the disguise had worked well. He tried to put himself in Silas's shoes. What would he do?

The answer was obvious. Silas would have to pass on the news that Arnie was still alive and the only person who might be interested was Lance Whittaker. Sharper was convinced there was a connection there between the killing of Sam and whatever was being cooked up by Whittaker.

He positioned himself on the opposite side of the street from Whittaker's office and started to roll a cigarette. The air was fresher now after the midday heat and a slight breeze added to the cooling effect. Lighting up, he inhaled deeply, watching the breeze sweep the smoke away in an instant. Whittaker's office door opened, and, well, well, well, Sharper thought, who should emerge but Silas Marsh. So there was a link, but what

Sharper couldn't figure out was, what was that link exactly?

Marsh walked down Main Street to the hitch-rail where his horse waited. Mounting up, he set off at a gentle trot out of town. Sharper wasted no time in heading for the livery. He had to get King saddled up and then follow Silas. He was convinced the deputy was heading for the other three men.

Silas Marsh was indeed on his way to warn his partners. But unbeknown to him, they had other plans. And those plans involved more killings.

Bart, with his foot bound, led Clem and Ben into town. Their objective was to eliminate the only witnesses, as far as they were concerned, that could identify them: Mick O'Hara, Des Malone and Abe Montana. Once that job was accomplished, their worries would be over.

Lance Whittaker had told the three where the men were staying, a run-down boarding-house on the outskirts of town where a lot of disillusioned miners hung out. They tethered their horses a block away and made their way to the boarding-house. Night was falling fast; already, tendrils of blood-red sunlight were fading as the sun dropped behind the foothills, casting long, eerie shadows.

Their aim was to stay hidden until the three men came out and then, using their knives, kill them as quietly as possible and get the hell back to their lair. The bushwhackers were almost taken by surprise as, within five minutes of arriving, their quarry left the boarding-house, making their way to the nearest saloon.

This part of the city was quiet and, best of all, dark. None of the sophistication of mid-town, where street lights lit up almost every nook and cranny; here it was shades of the Old West, not quite lawless, but both the sheriff's and marshal's officers rarely made sorties here after dark.

Clem was the first with his knife out. The first man to go down was Des Malone. He uttered a low groan and slumped to the dirt. It was then that Clem, Bart and Ben were taken by surprise. Abe Montana and Mick O'Hara drew their six-guns and started firing randomly, neither being sure exactly where the attack had come from. They got lucky. Clem got caught in the arm, his throwing arm, by a .45 slug. He let out an involuntary yell as he gripped his arm, thereby giving their position away.

There was no need for silence now. The thunder of the six-guns echoed all around as the two remaining cowboys continued firing. The shots were now returned by Bart and Ben. Gunsmoke filled the small street and the men's ears rang from the loud cracks as each shot was fired. It soon became obvious to Bart that they had reached an impasse. 'Let's get outa here, it just ain't working,' he said to Ben.

'Come on Clem, we're getting out. Now!' Ben said.

'I'll cover you,' Bart almost whispered. 'Bring my horse as close as you can, this foot is killing me.'

Ben helped Clem to get to the horses. 'How's the arm?'

'Sore as all hell,' came the reply.

'I'll take a look when we get back to the cabin,' Ben assured him.

Once mounted, Ben led Bart's horse closer to him and half-whispered, 'Bart, behind you.'

The shots were still coming thick and fast, most thudding into the clapboard fronts of surrounding buildings or sending up sand as slugs plunged into the hard-packed earth. Bart started backing up, still firing, and reached his mount. The three quickly made their exit and headed back into the foothills.

The firing continued for a few minutes after they'd left, until Mick and Abe realized their attackers had vamoosed.

'Go get the doc,' Abe said to Mick. 'Des is still alive!'

Silas reached the ridge that overlooked the cabin. There were no lights, horses or any signs of life. He paused there for a while, wondering what to do. Silas was a slow, cautious man, not one to make quick decisions, and sometimes, he made no decisions at all. He was good at doing what he was told to do, but weak on making up his own mind.

Eventually, he convinced himself there was nobody around and decided he might just as well ride back to town. In a flash of unexpected deduction, he figured that, as he hadn't passed his partners in crime on the way out here, they must have used the old trail into town. Turning his horse, Silas decided to ride back to town down the old trail in the hope of maybe finding sign of the men he sought.

Sharper was a good ten minutes behind Silas. His tracks were getting more difficult to follow as night fell. The cloudy sky was obscuring the moon, so the light was very faint. The ground was becoming rockier and pretty soon there were no tracks at all. Sharper had to follow his instincts as the trail wound its way gently up into the foothills. Reining in, he thought he heard the sound of iron striking rock and turned his head left and right, trying to determine where the sound came from.

He waited.

The noise came again, but it was too faint to determine a direction; the surrounding hills reflected the sound so it could have come from anywhere. Gently kicking King's flanks, he walked on, climbing higher into the foothills until he reached a ridge.

The clouds parted and the full moon shone its ghostly blue-white light over the terrain. Sharper sat atop his mount and took out his tobacco pouch. Rolling a quirly, he closed his eyes and struck a match on his thumb and lit up; he didn't want to ruin his night vision in the glare of the flaming match. All the while his ears were finely tuned to any sound.

There was none. The utter silence at times seemed deafening after the hustle and bustle of Virginia City. Flicking the match to the ground, he inhaled deeply and opened his eyes.

It was then he saw the cabin.

As Silas before him, he saw no signs of life and dismissed it from his mind. The foothills were full of small makeshift cabins of all shapes and sizes, as well as tents from back East and in dire cases, just a tarp on poles to keep the rain out. Sharper realized it was pointless carrying on in the dark and, finishing his cigarette, he wheeled King around and set off back down the trail he'd come by, unaware of a second trail.

Arriving back in town, Sharper decided to call in on Doc James to see how Arnie was getting on. Knocking on the surgery door, it was opened by the doc's nurse who stood aside so he could enter.

'Sorry to disturb you, ma'am, just wonderin'

how Arnie is doing?' Sharper said, taking off his Stetson.

'Doctor James is out on a call at the moment. There was a gunfight at the edge of town and a man was stabbed,' the nurse replied.

'Another stabbing!' Sharper was more than curious. 'Where was this?' he asked.

'The Old House boarding-house. Follow Main Street to the end and turn left, it's about two blocks down,' she said.

'And Arnie?' Sharper inquired.

'Arnie is still under sedation, but he's doing fine so far,' the nurse went on. 'It was touch and go for a while – there was quite a lot of internal bleeding – but he's a strong, young boy. Doctor James feels he'll pull through.'

'That's good news, I'll call back in the morning; it's important I get to talk to him,' Sharper said. 'Once again, sorry to disturb you, ma'am.'

'Not a problem, Mr Sharper,' the nurse smiled, She opened the door for him and, donning his Stetson, Sharper left to find Doc James.

He followed the nurse's directions and soon found the doc. Two or three men were standing with torches around the doc and the body of a man slumped on the floor. As Sharper approached, Doc James was just pulling an eight-inch throwing knife from the man's stomach. Blood oozed from the wound, but not in gushing spurts as Sharper thought it might. The man winced. Sharper immediately recognized him as one of the three who'd been duped.

'So he's alive then?' Sharper said.

'Yeah, he'll be fine,' the doc replied.

'Any idea who did this?' Sharper asked the man.

'Nah, was too – too – dark,' the man replied, obviously in pain.

Sharper took the knife from the doc and studied it.

'Could this be the same sort of knife that was used on Arnie, Doc?' he asked.

'Well, the wounds are similar, I'd say. If it weren't this knife it was surely one very like it,' the doc replied.

'I'll hand this in to Sheriff Prady,' Sharper said.

The doc didn't answer, just continued to minister to his patient. When he was satisfied, he got some of the bystanders to lift the man on to his over-used stretcher. 'Let's get him back to the surgery,' he said. 'All he needs now is rest.'

Sharper watched the men troop off. His mind was a whirl of thoughts. This was no random attack, and no coincidence either. It all pointed to the men who had slugged him on his first night in town, and Sharper was determined to bring those thugs to justice. He pocketed the knife and, picking up one of the discarded torches, began to take a look round the street that was actually more of a large alleyway. He saw scuffed boot prints that were recent near one of the buildings and, on closer inspection he found blood. So, one of the bushwhackers was hit, he thought. That's good news. Should slow 'em down a tad.

Under cover of the dark night, as the clouds moved in again, Ben Doyle returned to the scene; Clem had demanded that he got his knife back. Staying in the shadows, Ben had watched as the stabbed man was carted off and saw the bearded figure pocket the throwing knife. Ben bided his time; the darkness was in his favour as he watched the man inspecting the ground, coming ever closer.

As Sharper knelt to feel the blood between his finger and thumb, Ben brought the butt of his gun down hard, catching Sharper on the back of the neck, knocking him out cold.

CHAPTER 8

Ben Doyle now made his way down to the surgery. There was unfinished business to attend to and he aimed to end it here and now. His plans were thwarted, however, as he saw the sheriff enter the surgery. Sneaking up to a side window, Ben peered through the glass to see three men in what appeared to be a waiting room: the sheriff and two of the fellas he and his pards had tricked out of their hard-earned dollars for a worthless claim. Not counting the doc, he made it odds of three to one; odds Ben did not care to take on.

Cursing his luck, Ben walked back to his patient horse and mounted up. At least he had recovered Clem's knife. They'd have to re-group and plan their next attack. Leaving town, Ben rode to the place they'd agreed to meet on the trail back to the cabin. Clem and Bart were waiting impatiently for news. The news they got did not please them.

'Seems to me,' Bart said, 'this whole scheme is about to go belly-up, less'n we get rid o' them witnesses.'

'I need a doc,' Clem said. 'This arm is sure sore.'

'Ben, you'll have to get one of the other docs in town to see to Clem. Don't matter which one, but you need to do it now.'

'Here's your knife,' Ben said, 'at least I got that back.'

Clem took his prized knife with his left hand and sheathed it without even a thanks.

'There's a cleft in the rocks yonder,' said Bart. 'We'll hole up there till you return.'

'It'll take a while,' Ben said, 'I'll have to go the long way round and enter town from the north. I'll get a doc, even if it's by force.'

Sharper eased himself up to a sitting position. He was getting a mite fed up of being slugged. His head throbbed and his eyesight was slightly blurry. He doubted he could stand yet, so he bided his time, waiting for the pain to ease. Feeling the back of his neck, he was relieved to see there was no bleeding. Eventually, he stood on legs that felt as if they belonged to someone else, and made his way back to Doc James's surgery. He was as sore as all hell, and not just in the head.

'Sharper? What the hell—' It was Sheriff Prady who spoke up.

'Yeah, yeah, I got slugged again,' Sharper responded. 'I found blood on the street, so one of 'em musta been hit, I got the kn—' he stopped short as he realized the throwing knife had been taken back.

'Goddamn! I had the knife!'

'Let's take a look at your head,' Doc James said, pushing his spectacles down on his nose. He poked and prodded for a while, then said, 'Skin ain't broken, but you'll sure have a sore head for a while.'

'Tell me something I don't know,' Sharper replied acidly.

'Hey, don't shoot the messenger,' Doc James said, affronted.

'Sorry, Doc, just getting a tad sore at being slugged in this damn place.'

'You find out where Silas went?' the sheriff asked.

'Nah, I followed the trail south, but it got too dark to see any sign.'

'Too bad,' Prady said, wistfully.

'I reckon whoever got shot is gonna need a doc,' Sharper said. 'How many are there in town?'

'Hell, there's at least six,' Doc James replied.

'Can't stake 'em all out,' Prady added.

'We gotta concentrate on Whittaker and Marsh,' Sharper said, 'They're our only connection to the three men.'

'Agreed,' said Prady.

'How's Arnie doin'?' Sharper asked.

'I'll keep him sedated until the morning,' the doc replied. 'He should be recovering fine by then.'

'Maybe he saw who killed Sam and tried to kill him.' Prady said.

'Let's hope so,' Sharper said. 'I figure this is all tied up with this scam, an' I aim to get to the bottom of it. And soon.'

It took Ben a good hour to reach town; the ride to the north end was longer than he thought. Riding down a side street, he spotted a sign swinging gently in the breeze: Jacob C. Christie MD.

Ben reined in and hitched his horse to the hitch-rail outside the doc's place. Although it was only nine o'clock, there were no lights showing in the house, but Ben knocked loudly on the white-painted front door. He waited impatiently for a few moments, then knocked again, and kept knocking until he saw the light of an oil lamp through one of the windows.

'All right, all right, I'm coming,' a voice rasped from the inside. The door opened a crack and a wizened face poke through. 'What do you want?' the doc asked.

'Got a shot man, Doc. You gotta come with me,' Ben said.

The old man replied, 'I ain't going anywhere,' and began to close the door, but Ben's foot blocked it and he drew his gun.

'I said you gotta come with me!' he repeated. He pushed hard on the door and knocked the old doc over in the process.

'Goddamn, you can't—' the doc stopped speaking as he caught sight of Ben's drawn pistol.

'Mr Colt here says I can,' Ben stated. 'Now get your bag, *pronto.*'

'At least let me dress and get the buggy ready,' the doc pleaded.

'Ain't got time for that,' Ben replied. 'You can double up on my mount. Now get your bag, an' bring that oil lamp, an' let's go!'

Grumbling, the old man got to his feet. He knew better than to argue the toss with a man holding a gun on him. Getting his bag, he tied up his dressing gown belt, shoved some shoes on and followed Ben out the door.

Ben decided not to return the way he had come; it was too long, so, keeping to the side streets, he made his way south and safely left town, the doc hanging on for grim life as Ben set the horse to a gallop.

It took only twenty minutes to reach the rendezvous point where Ben reined in. He dismounted and helped the old man off his horse and ushered him towards Clem.

'Thanks for coming out, Doc,' Clem said.

'Had no choice in that,' the doc replied.

The doc knelt by Clem's side and lit the oil lamp. 'Let's take a look at you,' he said. 'Where were you hit?'

'Right arm, Doc. It sure hurts some,' Clem replied.

Doc Christie opened his bag, took out a pair of scissors and began to cut the sleeve from Clem's right arm so he could get a look at the wound.

'You were lucky, Mr—'

'Name's not important,' Clem said. 'Lucky?'

'Just a wing shot – hit your tricep so the bullet ain't in there. I'll apply some antiseptic, bind your arm and give you a dose of laudanum. That should help.'

Clem was silent as the antiseptic was applied. It stung like hell, but Clem was determined not to show it.

'That should stop infection,' the doc said. 'I think I'll need to put a few stitches there, it'll help the wound heal quicker.'

Sweat was pouring down Clem's face, but he just nodded.

'Here, take a swig of this, it'll help numb the pain.' Doc Christie handed Clem a bottle of laudanum, which Clem gratefully took, downing two big slugs of the liquid. The doc inserted six stitches in the arm, but the laudanum had taken effect within minutes and Clem was so relaxed the doc could have sawn his arm off for all he cared. Binding the wound with a bandage, the doc stood and said, 'That'll do it. Now take me back to town, if you please.'

'Well, we got a problem there, Doc,' Ben said.

'You don't expect me to walk!' the doc exploded.

'Oh, no, Doc, we don't expect that,' Ben drawled and smiled.

Suddenly the doc began to sweat as he realized they were not going to let him go. Ben drew his Colt, and from a distance of no more than two feet, shot the doc in the temple. The blast shattered the silence and reverberated off rocks and echoed for an amazingly long time. The doc was flung back as if hit by a bull. Bone, blood and brain sprayed through the air and most of it seemed to hit Clem like sticky goo. The doc's body thudded to the ground and shook for several seconds as his body realized it was dead.

Then he stopped moving.

'Jeez, Ben, I'm covered in brain stuff,' Clem wailed.

'Better'n dying from infection,' Ben said as he re-holstered his six-gun. 'Come on, mount up and let's get outa here.'

'Bring that bag with you,' Clem said. 'I might need some more medicine.'

*

It was next morning when a distraught female burst into Sheriff Prady's office.

'Sheriff, Sheriff, the doctor's gone missing! I came in to work today and the office door was open and there was no sign of him. You've got to do something quickly – he could be in danger!'

'Whoa! Hold on there, young lady,' Prady said placatingly. 'Take a seat and start at the beginning. Now, which doc are we talkin' about?'

The young woman, who turned out to be a nurse, sat down in the proffered chair, her hands knotted together and her face filled with concern. 'Doctor Christie,' she said.

'And you say the door was open?'

'Yes, and no sign of the doctor.'

'Could be he was called out on an emergency,' Prady said.

'He always left a note if he left the office. Always. He always kept me informed of his whereabouts. This is not like him at all. His bag has gone, but his clothes are where he left them in his bedroom; he's a man of routine.'

'Hmm,' Prady mused.

'The horse and buggy are still there, Sheriff, so I know he didn't go out on a call. You've got to help me!' the woman pleaded.

'Don't worry, ma'am, I'll organize a search party.

We'll soon sort this matter out. Now you go back to the office and wait there, in case he returns. OK?'

'Yes, Sheriff, good idea. I'll go straight there now,' she replied and hurriedly left the office.

As she left, Sharper entered.

'How's the head?' Prady asked.

'Throbbing,' Sharper replied. 'Can I help myself to some coffee?'

'Sure, pour me one, too.'

'Who was the woman?' Sharper asked as he sat down.

'Seems ol' Doc Christie has gone missing. I'm gonna form a search party. You want to maybe ride along?' Prady asked.

'Don't you see what this means?' Sharper said, exasperated.

'Cain't say I rightly do,' Prady replied.

'The blood I found in the alley didn't come from the stabbed man,' Sharper began. 'One of the bushwhackers was hit, Sheriff. He needed a doc!'

'By hell! You're right. Well, we better get some men together; we'll split 'em into two search parties. I'll take the main trail and you take the old trail. OK?'

'Old trail?' Sharper queried.

'Yeah, sure. There's two trails heading south from this part of town,' the sheriff informed him. 'No one uses the old trail much these days; it's far

easier to get to the gold and silver claims by following the new trail – quicker too.'

'That accounts for me missing Silas then,'
Sharper said. 'He must have returned to town on
the old trail. Dammit!'

'Come to think of it,' Prady said, 'I ain't seen
hide nor hair of Silas.'

'Don't surprise me none,' Sharper said. 'He's
either met up with his buddies or—' A sudden
thought hit Sharper right between the eyes. 'If he
missed his buddies on the trail, then there's only
one place he'd head,' Sharper said.

'Lance Whittaker!' Both men said the name at
the same time.

Silas March had indeed gone straight to Lance
Whittaker.

He was a worried man. It seemed the killing was
going to go on and on, and this was not the way
Silas had wanted things to go. While his conscience allowed swindling losers out of their
money to earn a few extra bucks, killing was something else. And Silas was now up to his neck in it.

'This is getting too heavy for me, Lance,' Silas
said.

'It's too late to back out now, Silas. You should
have thought about this before you agreed to
help,' Lance replied.

'I didn't reckon on killin' anyone. What the hell

did they kill the Chinese for? They weren't on no claim.'

'That was a bad error of judgement,' Lance replied dismissively.

'*Error of judgement*! They're plain loco. They killed ol' Sam, and tried to kill Arnie and one of the fellas we duped. How many more they gonna kill? You? Me?' Silas flopped down into a chair.

'Here,' Lance said, 'have a drink and calm down.'

Silas accepted the shot glass and downed it in one gulp. The smooth whisky, imported from Scotland, did not allay his fears or appease his conscience.

'It's got to stop, Lance. If'n it don't I'm gonna come clean with Sheriff Prady.'

'You do that and we'll all swing at the end of a rope,' Lance warned.

'I'll take my chances,' Silas answered and held his glass out for a refill.

Lance took his glass and walked over to the drinks cabinet. Lifting a brass candlestick, he returned to Silas's side, handed him the drink and brought the candlestick down on his head.

Hard.

Silas slumped in the chair, still holding his glass. Lance stayed still for a few moments, waiting to see if the man moved. Then, gingerly, he felt for a pulse. He felt none, but leaned in close to the deputy's face to see if he was breathing.

Silas March was as dead as a slaughtered steer. All Lance had to do now was get rid of the body. But that was no easy task. Silas was a big, heavy man and Lance was a fat, soft lawyer. There was no way he could tote that hunk anywhere. What to do? he thought. He couldn't leave Silas in the chair sitting in the middle of his office; he certainly couldn't risk trying to drag him outside and it would be impossible to lift the big man on to his buggy.

Lance then decided on a plan. He pulled an old Indian rug across the floor and placed it in front of the chair. Then, lifting the back of the chair and pushing it forward, he used all of his strength, which wasn't much, to tilt it forwards so that Silas's body fell face down on the rug.

Lance Whittaker was panting, he was red with exertion, and sweat ran down his body. He walked to his own chair and sat, taking out a handkerchief to mop his face. Breathing hard, he gulped down his glass of whisky to calm his nerves and get his breath back. Eventually, he stood, pulled down his fancy jacket, and returned to the body. Rolling the rug, he wrapped Silas's body in it and manoeuvred it to the rear of his office, so it was at least partly hidden by his desk.

He had to get to Bart and the boys now; they would have to dispose of the late deputy. That meant a trip out to the cabin. Something he'd

113

managed to avoid – until now. Dousing the lamps, Lance left his office, carefully pulling down the blinds and locking the door. Satisfied that nothing looked untoward, he walked to the back of his office, hitched up the pony to his buggy and set off, pleased that so far all was well.

CHAPTER 9

Sharper left the sheriff's office and made his way back to the boarding-house where he knew Mick O'Hara and Abe Montana were staying. He felt sure they'd want to ride the trail with him. His instincts had been right. After explaining the situation, the two men were only too willing to help. 'Good men,' Sharper said. 'Meet me in front of the sheriff's office in thirty minutes.'

The plan was agreed.

Waiting with Prady, Sharper got the directions to hit the old trail. He checked his Smith & Wesson, then his Winchester, making sure he had plenty of ammunition. Although he didn't expect any gunplay, it was better to be prepared. Almost to the minute, both Mick and Abe showed up, closely followed by two men Sharper didn't recognize.

'Here's my two men as well,' Prady said. 'OK,

let's hit the trail and see what we can find.'

The six men mounted up and prepared to go their separate ways.

'The two trails meet up at the topmost ridge in the foothills, about eight or nine miles on my trail. Yours is a tad longer, Sharper, maybe twelve miles. We'll wait for you there. If either of us finds anything, one man stays put and the other two wait at the ridge, OK?'

The men nodded and the two search parties set off.

Prady's directions were very accurate and Sharper and his two cohorts soon found themselves outside of Virginia City, heading south on a trail that had nearly returned to nature. Sharper kept his eyes peeled for any sign that might be fresh. There had been no rain, so any hoof prints within the last twenty-four hours would be clearly visible.

Although not used much these days, Sharper was surprised at the number of tracks he could see – both coming and going into town. While he kept his gaze on the trail, Mick scanned left and Abe right; if there was anything to see, they had the terrain pretty well covered.

Walking their mounts, so as not to miss anything, the trio plodded onwards. The trail was beginning to rise now, as the distant foothills loomed into sight. Overhead, the sun showed it was about mid-morning and the warmth was welcome now, though later the warmth would turn to heat as the ground heated up, and waves of hot air would make the going almost intolerable.

Approaching an outcrop of rock, Sharper called a halt. Something had caught his eye. The hard-packed soil had changed to softer sand at this point and sign was clearly visible. 'Looks like three or four hoof prints here,' Sharper said and dismounted for a closer inspection. Abe and Mick joined him. 'Two of the tracks are the same horse,' Sharper said. 'See the damaged right front hoof?'

Both men nodded in agreement.

'One of 'em seems to be a mighty heavy horse,' Abe observed.

'Either that, or it had two men on its back,' Sharper said, and gave both men a knowing look. Following the tracks ahead, they veered to the right as they reached the outcrop. Leaving their horses ground-hitched, the three men drew their weapons and walked on. Placing themselves up tight against the rock face, Sharper peered into the recess in the rock which turned out to be much larger than he'd first thought.

It was then he saw the body. Beckoning Abe and Mick, they entered the recess and went straight to the body lying on its back at the far end.

'You recognize him?' Sharper asked.

Both men shook their heads. The man was

117

wearing long johns and a dressing-gown; hardly the garb of a volunteer.

'I reckon we found the doc,' Sharper said. Kneeling down, he saw the neat hole in the man's forehead. Traces of black powder covered his face, along with a swarm of flies, and already the smell of death was turning into a stench.

'Shot close range,' Sharper said, 'poor bastard didn't have a chance.'

'Look here,' Abe shouted, and pointed to a shirt sleeve.

Sharper picked the blood-soaked sleeve up. 'Makes sense, now don't it. You winged one of the bushwhackers and they needed a doc.'

'They didn't have to kill him,' Abe said, in a low voice.

'They did,' Sharper said, 'otherwise it's another witness.'

'How many do they have to kill?' Mick asked.

'These men have no conscience,' Sharper said, 'and with Silas March and Lance Whittaker pretending to keep it all legal, they think they're in the clear. But they made two big mistakes.'

'And they were?' Abe asked.

'They killed two innocent Chinese for the hell of it and they slugged me!' Sharper moved away from the body and surveyed the ground behind it: bone, blood and gore, covered in flies, was splattered along the ground and then up against rocks.

Grey matter clung there in sickly globs as the feeding frenzy continued. Sharper felt sick to the stomach.

'You want me to stay here while you ride to the ridge?' Mick asked.

'No, you two appraise Prady of what we've found. I'll stay here in case they come back for this piece of evidence,' Sharper said.

Nodding, Abe and Mick left the recess and rose up the trail at a steady gallop.

Lance Whittaker had reached the crest of the ridge without encountering any problems. He guided the buggy down the slope to the disused line cabin and parked at the rear. His approach had been closely watched by the three men inside, so his knock on the door came as no surprise.

'We got a problem, boys,' Lance began. 'Marsh was threatening to come clean to the sheriff, I had no choice.'

'Damn an' hell,' Bart said. 'He was our tame official when we produced fake title deeds, "enforcing" the law!'

'Well, now we need a new law enforcer,' Whittaker said. 'Thing is, his body is wrapped in a rug in my office, he's too big for me to cart out.' Then he noticed Clem's arm. 'What in hell happened to you?'

Clem explained what had happened in town,

but omitted to tell Whittaker of the doc's fate.

'That was a dumb move,' Whittaker said. 'We got enough on our plate without you risking the operation.'

'Them three fellas are waitin' for us. We can't go into town unless we get rid of 'em,' Bart said.

'Well we need to get rid of that body,' Whittaker said. He took out a cigar, bit the end off and spat it to the floor. The three men remained silent while he puffed the cigar into life.

'You'll have to come in after dark,' Whittaker said. 'I'll keep the office locked until then.'

'You'll have to give us a hand,' Bart said. 'Clem's useless and I got me a bad foot.'

'I'll be there,' Whittaker said. 'Just make sure you are! I'll keep the lights off. Knock four times,' he rapped his knuckles on the table in an even tempo, 'just like that and I'll know it's you.'

'Keep that fancy buggy o' yours handy,' Ben said. 'We'll use it to dump the body.'

'It'll be ready,' Whittaker replied. 'Now I must get back to town.'

Without further ado, Whittaker left and set off back to his office.

More by luck than good management, not only had Whittaker avoided running into one of the search parties driving out to the cabin, but by the time he set off, Abe and Mick had found the sheriff, and had ridden back down the old trail to the scene of the murder.

'That's Doc Christie all right,' Prady said as he kneeled by the body.

'I figure one of the bushwhackers rode back into town and brought the doc out here by force,' Sharper said. 'He was yet another witness, and he had to die.'

'I still don't see how the Chinese fit into all this,' Prady said.

'They don't. These men just like killing. Soo Lee and her grandfather just happened to be in the wrong place at the wrong time,' Sharper said.

'Right,' Prady said, 'let's get the doc back to town and go see Arnie and, what's his name?'

'Malone,' Abe said. 'Des Malone.'

'Yeah, him. Seems to me you three fellas and possible Arnie are also witnesses and as such—'

'They'll try and kill us?' Mick interjected.

'That's for sure,' Prady said. 'We need to get them guarded securely as them two are the only ones who are vulnerable right now.'

'We can do that,' Mick said. 'After all, Des is our partner.'

' 'Preciate that,' Prady said, 'I'll swear you in as deputies when we get back.'

'No need fer that, Sheriff,' Abe said, 'we'd do it willingly.'

'I figured on that,' Bill Prady smiled. 'But let's keep this legal an' above board. If it comes to a shoot-out, I want you boys covered, OK?'

'Fair enough,' Mick said.

They lashed Doc Christie to Abe's horse, and he doubled up with Mick for the ride back to town.

Lance Whittaker parked the buggy behind his office and hooked a bag of oats over the horse's nose to keep it happy, until night came. He walked to the front of his office, scanning the street to see if anyone was watching. When he was sure no one was, he unlocked the door and quickly stepped inside, locking it behind him. Although bright sunshine outside, with the blinds down, the office was dark and gloomy and a smell filled the air that made him gag as he entered.

He grabbed the bottle of imported whisky and, removing his jacket and hanging it up neatly, slumped in his chair. He poured three fingers and gulped it in one go and poured another. All he had to do now was wait.

Reaching Doc James's surgery, the men dismounted. Sharper turned to Abe and asked him to fetch the undertaker. Abe scurried off. Sheriff Prady knocked on the door and Doc James opened it toting a handgun.

'You had trouble, Doc?' Prady asked.

'Nope, but I was ready for it if it came.' The old man smiled and gave Prady a wink.

'Get some coffee on, please, Sadie,' the doc said to his nurse. 'We could be in for a long day.'

Between them, Sharper and Prady explained what was going on, as far as they knew, and assured the doc that both Abe and Mick would be there to guard Arnie and Des Malone.

'We got ol' Doc Christie outside,' Prady added. 'They done killed him, too.'

'He was a good man,' Doc James said, 'a damn good man.'

A knock on the door made the men jump. Sharper drew his Smith & Wesson and went to open it. Abe stood there with Barney Gilpin, the undertaker, who seemed to be almost gleeful at another funeral – especially one that would be paid for privately.

'I'll take good care of him.' Barney said and, with his assistant, took down Christie's body and placed it in his curtained hearse. Waving, the undertaker drove off.

Abe closed the door and they made plans for the safekeeping of both Arnie and Des. They moved both patients to the centre of the house. Abe was to guard the front, and Mick the back. There were no other entries to the property, so they felt secure enough.

'I'm going to see if I can find Silas and Lance,' Sharper said. 'They might not be involved in any gunplay, but I think it better they were behind bars. What do you think, Bill?'

'I think I better swear you three fellas in as deputies now, that's what I think,' the sheriff said.

The sheriff performed the brief ceremony and, with Abe and Mick set in their places, Sharper left for Lance Whittaker's office while the sheriff went back to his own office to get some deputy badges and see if Silas had turned up.

The late afternoon sun seemed to have lost none of its heat as Sharper made his way along the street. He was conscious of the heat coming up from the hard-packed earth beneath his feet and there was not a breath of wind. At this time of day, the heat was stifling and uncomfortable. Crossing the busy street, Sharper stood on the boardwalk opposite Whittaker's office. He leaned on a wooden pillar and rolled a cigarette as he studied the building opposite. There seemed to be no signs of life there; the blinds were drawn and no light came from inside.

Sharper was a patient man and was prepared to stay there all night if necessary, but it seemed pointless to hang around on the off chance of some action. He crossed the street and tried the door. It was locked, of course. Placing a hand on the glass to shield the glare of the sun, Sharper tried to peer inside, but the blinds fitted too well and revealed nothing of the interior. It would be prematurely dark soon as the sun began to dip in the western sky behind the distant mountains.

A blood-red glow bathed the town, creating eerie shadows that grew longer as he watched. For a moment, Sharper thought of breaking into the office, but dismissed the idea as it would be a give-away that someone was on to Whittaker's case. So he crossed back over the street and hung around for a few more minutes.

And waited.

Sheriff Prady unlocked the door of his office, already knowing that his deputy had not returned there. He opened the bottom drawer of his desk and rummaged around for deputy badges, found them and slipped them into his breast pocket. He'd argue the toss with the town council later. He sat at his desk and took out his pipe. Slowly and methodically, he cleared out the bowl and refilled it with tobacco. He put the pipe in his mouth, but didn't light it yet. It was all part of a ritual he went through to both calm his nerves and think.

Back at the line cabin, Bart and Ben finished cleaning their weapons. They checked the loads of the handguns and rifles, and then took their time rolling a cigarette. Ben filled three shot glasses with whiskey and they, too, waited.

Clem sat flexing the fingers of his left hand and,

although his arm was uncomfortable, he was more peeved at not being able to get back to town and finish this business once and for all. 'I could shoot with my left hand,' he stated, out of the blue. 'Better the three of us, than just two,' he added. He stared out of the smear-stained window through which the diminishing sunlight filtered and seethed.

He'd get his revenge – one way or another.

And soon.

CHAPTER 10

Although Whittaker's appearance was that of a soft, fat man, he had the constitution of an ox. Nothing seemed to rattle him, and he knew that the only way out of their predicament, and to maintain their steady and considerable income, was to kill anyone who recognized his partners. So far he was convinced that no one had any inkling that he was involved in any nefarious scheme and felt he could act with impunity.

Little did he know that he was wrong about that.

Even his implacable resolve was beginning to wilt with the waiting. He glanced at the rolled up Indian rug in the far corner of the room, seeing for the first time, boots hanging out of one end. Grabbing the fine whisky bottle again, he poured another shot and held the glass for a moment, before downing its contents.

He reached into his vest pocket and pulled out his gold savonnette Hunter, flipped open the lid to disclose the brilliant white face. He studied the Roman numerals and watched as the second hand moved around the dial. Of all his possessions, this was his favourite – the sign of a wealthy man; a man with power and substance. He closed the lid, hearing the always satisfying solid click, and placed the watch back in his vest pocket, then adjusted the chain so it hung perfectly. He didn't notice the time; that was unimportant. Just looking at the watch reminded him of his position.

'Another little tipple,' he said aloud to himself and poured a larger measure this time.

It was then he made a mistake.

Opening the humidor on his desk, he removed a Cuban cigar, rolled it between thumb and forefinger, by his left ear, then slid it under his nose, inhaling the delicate aroma of the tobacco. He took out the clippers and neatly chopped off one end. Placing it between his teeth, he reached for the long matches and struck it on the rough surface specially designed for the purpose at the side of the humidor.

The match flared, seeming to light up the whole room, but Whittaker didn't notice that as, surrounded by his favourite whisky, his Hunter and his desk, he revelled in the delight of lighting the cigar. He inhaled the delicious-smelling smoke and breathed out contentedly. All was, or would be, well with the world. His world.

Sharper was about to leave when something caught his eye. It lasted for only a few seconds, and made him wonder if he was seeing things. A small flash of light had escaped through the blinds of Whittaker's office.

So he's in there! Sharper thought. But why is he in the dark? It doesn't make sense, unless. . . . The 'unless' became obvious now, Whittaker was waiting for someone, but who? Silas? The three bushwhacking murderers? His suspicions that things were coming to a head were maybe correct. . . .

Sharper decided he'd better warn Abe and Mick, and then Sheriff Prady. As far as he was aware, the doc's place was the obvious target as it contained the men who recognized them. Stubbing out his third cigarette, he made his way to Doc James's surgery.

He knocked on the door to be asked, 'Who's there?'

'It's me, Sharper.'

The door opened slightly and Abe's face appeared, making sure it was Sharper, then it swung wide open to allow him to enter.

'Whittaker's in his office, sitting in the dark,' Sharper began. 'I think he's waiting for his men to come into town.'

'I think you should listen to what Arnie has to say,' Doc James said. 'The laudanum's worn off and he's coherent now,' he added.

Sharper listened quietly as Arnie told his story of what had happened at one of the claim sites.

'Did you tell Sam?' Sharper asked.

'Sure, an' we went to the sheriff's office to tell him, too.'

Sharper's face showed consternation. 'You told the sheriff?'

'No, he wasn't there, but we told the deputy, Silas Marsh,' Arnie replied, wincing slightly as he lifted his head, then slowly lowered it again.

'You rest up now, Arnie,' Sharper said.

Outside, in the corridor, Sharper said, 'Well that solves one mystery. Now we know why Sam was killed and why Arnie got hisself stabbed, too.'

'What you figure they're gonna do now?' Abe asked.

'I reckon they're getting desperate now,' Sharper replied. 'They've failed to kill Arnie and Des, and you two are still here, so I figure they're going to attack here. And soon.'

'Hell, we can hold off two gunnies and a cripple,' Mick said, with bravado.

'Maybe,' Sharper said. 'Maybe you can, maybe not. How much ammo you got?'

'Got me a belt-full o' .45s,' Abe said.

'Me too,' Mick added.

'We'll need more. I'm going to get Sheriff Prady and raid his arsenal.'

Sharper turned to leave, when Doc James said, 'You think we should get more men?'

'Way I figure it, Doc,' Sharper said, 'we don't want to attract any more attention than we have to. Any suspicion they might have that we're ready for them and they'll vamoose, as sure as eggs is eggs, and we might not get a second chance to nail 'em.'

It seemed to make sense to the doc, but Sharper could see the man was worried.

'Don't worry, Doc, they might think they have the element of surprise, but in fact it's us that do.' Sharper smiled and that seemed to placate the doc.

Leaving the surgery, Sharper made his way to the sheriff's office and told Prady the whole story.

'So you see, I reckon Doc James's place will be the target. And it'll happen tonight.' Sharper waited while Prady collected his thoughts.

'OK, I agree,' the sheriff said after careful consideration. 'Having more men would only attract attention and, as you say, the element of surprise is with us. I got plenty of ammo here, and four brand new Winchesters. We'll take them over now.'

With Sharper carrying the four rifles and Prady the ammunition – all .45 calbre – Prady locked the office door and they set off the hundred yards or so to Doc James's surgery. Once inside, they sorted

131

their defences out. It was agreed that Doc James would stay in the room with Arnie and Des.

'I got my old Navy Colt,' the doc said, 'just in case.'

'Hope you won't need it, Doc,' Sharper said.

Prady and Mick were at the back of the house, each armed with two revolvers and a rifle and with enough ammunition to hold off a small army. Abe took the front of the building. As it was felt that any attack would likely come from the rear, where it was out of public view, at the first sign of any disturbance he could be with Mick and Bill in seconds. Sharper had decided he would stake out the office of Lance Whittaker.

Light was failing fast now. Only the top of the sun was visible as it sank behind the mountain range in the far distance. The sky acquired a purplish haze and already the temperature began to plummet.

Sharper stood his ground on the opposite side of the street to Whittaker's office. He rested the Winchester against a clapboard wall and started to roll a cigarette when a voice behind him almost made him drop his makings.

'Brung ya some coffee.'

Sharper swung round, Smith & Wesson drawn and cocked.

'Goddamn, Harvey, don't sneak up on me like that. I coulda killed you!'

'Sorry, I didn't mean to sneak up. Saw you out here and figured you was checking out on fat boy over yonder,' Harvey said.

'I am, an' you better make yourself scarce, Harvey. There's something going down here tonight,' Sharper said, and he sipped the welcome coffee.

'On my way. You know where I am if'n you need me,' Harvey said and walked back to his shop.

'Let's get goin',' Bart said.

Ben, the only fully fit man amongst them, helped Clem into the saddle. Bart mounted up on the right side of his horse, to save putting all his weight on his still-sore left foot.

The night air was mild and, unusually, the sky was near-cloudless, allowing the ghostly moon to light up the landscape, casting an eerie blue-white glow. Not that the three men noticed any of this. They concentrated on the trail up to the ridge and then down the other side, heading for Virginia City. Using the old trail, although a longer route, would bring them into the less salubrious part of town, where folks kept themselves to themselves and no one asked any questions.

They rode along in silence, knowing that tonight would either make or break them. Once you got the taste of money, you wanted more and more. Their stash of stolen gold, in nugget and dust form, was carefully hidden and was their ticket out of here if things went wrong. And in the dangerous environment in which they operated, anything could go wrong at any time.

Picking their way carefully down the trail, they neared the outskirts of town and reined in. It was Ben who offered a plan: 'I figure you two should wait at the back of ol' Whittaker's office while I sort out Silas.'

'I got a better idea,' Bart Sampson interjected. Me an' Clem'll hit the doc's place. We need to sort this out once an' for all. You join us when you've loaded up Silas.

'Get Whittaker to take the buggy and we'll meet him along the trail.'

'Maybe this time we'll kill all the birds with one stone,' Clem remarked drily.

Ben made his way to Whittaker's office. As instructed, he knocked carefully, four times.

Sharper was immediately alert.

After a few seconds, the door to Whittaker's office opened, and Ben slipped inside. Once the door was closed and locked, Ben explained the plan to Whittaker, who was none too pleased with having to dispose of the body by himself.

'Open that rear window,' Ben ordered, 'and we'll slide the body through it. I'll get outside as well and load it on to the buggy. Can you handle that?'

'Sure,' Whittaker replied, 'but there's no way I can get through that window.'

'Hell no,' Ben said with a grin etched on his face. 'You meet me round back, OK?'

Between them, they lifted the rug into a standing position and leant it on the window frame. Ben climbed out and Whittaker lifted the bottom end while Ben took the full weight on his broad shoulders and bundled it on the buggy.

'OK,' Ben whispered, 'it's loaded. Get your ass back here and wait for us on the trail where we agreed.'

Whittaker mumbled a reply and closed the window.

So, Sharper thought, Whittaker was in there and had obviously been waiting for a visit. From his position across the street, he could not positively identify the visitor, but from the way he was behaving, Sharper was sure it was one of the men he was looking for. Fifteen minutes passed before the door opened again.

But Sharper hadn't expected the man who appeared in the moonlight to be Lance Whittaker himself! He watched as the man carefully locked the door to his office and waddled his way along the boardwalk to the side alley and disappeared down it.

What the hell? Sharper thought. Why lock the

man inside? Unless. . . . There must be a way out back. But why not use the front door?

Sharper crossed the street, drawing his Smith & Wesson as he made his way to the alleyway. Stopping short, he peered into the dark alley. The buildings either side blocked out any moonlight and the street torches didn't shine this far, so Sharper could see nothing. But he heard low voices and then a horse trotting off, followed by the creaks and groans of a buckboard or similar.

He raced down the alleyway but he was too late. A rider had gone left, and the wheel tracks showed the buckboard had gone right. Without a horse he was stymied. But there was no time to get to the livery, saddle up and catch either man. Making a quick decision, he turned left as he suddenly thought: the surgery!

Bart and Clem hitched their horses in a side street a block down from the surgery. Bart helped Clem down. 'You sure you're up to this?' he asked.

'I got me an arm I can use,' Clem replied testily.

Picking their way through the darkness, the two men approached the surgery from the rear. Their plan was simple: break in, kill the occupants with knives, and get out as fast as possible. With the element of surprise on their side, they couldn't possible fail.

They thought.

Creeping to the back yard of the surgery, they paused and scanned the building. Clem already had his knife out, clutched in his left hand, as they peered over the small fence surrounding the house.

No lights showed.

'Figure the doc's out?' Bart said.

'Could be,' Clem replied in a whisper.

'Ben should be here soon, then we can make our move,' Bart said.

'We don't have to wait for him! We can handle this ourselves,' Clem said in annoyance. 'We ain't that crippled!'

'Let's stick to the plan,' Bart said.

Reluctantly, Clem agreed.

Sharper moved cautiously through the back alleys, his gun still drawn. He knew he was nearing the surgery, but didn't know the town's layout to be certain of exactly where he was. He stopped and listened. Not a sound; the area was eerily quiet. It seemed that no living soul was anywhere around. Then he heard the sound of a horse snorting, followed by a pawing on the ground.

Straining his ears, Sharper located the direction and crept forward. It must be the horse he'd seen leaving Whittaker's place. He was right; he recognized the bay instantly. So they aimed to hit the doc's, just as he thought.

But where were the other two men?

Suddenly, Sharper heard the metallic click of a gun being cocked. The noise seemed to echo unusually loudly in the silence of the evening air. A shot rang out so close that the smell of sulphur from black powder filled Sharper's nostrils. Instinctively, he dropped flat and rolled over, his Smith & Wesson seeking a target.

A second shot came, kicking up a plume of dust not two feet away from where Sharper lay. This time, he had seen a muzzle flash and he fired off two shots in quick succession.

'What the hell!' Abe Montana yelled as he heard the gunfire. He peered through the front window, but could see nothing. The shots brought Sheriff Prady running through from the back of the surgery.

'See anything?' he asked.

'Not a damn thing. You think it's them?' Abe asked.

'Maybe,' Prady answered. 'Sharper's out there, so we'll soon find out.'

A slug burst through the window, glass shattering everywhere. Luckily, the bullet passed between the two men who immediately ducked low, their guns ready.

'I think that answers your question,' Prady said, laconically.

'Where the hell's Sharper then?' Abe asked.

Prady didn't answer, but fired off a couple of random shots, to let whoever was shooting at them know they were ready.

'Goddammit!' Bart said, through gritted teeth. 'If that's Ben, he'll get the whole town round here now!'

'What'll we do now?' Clem asked.

'We wait,' came the terse reply from Bart. 'We ain't in no condition to go charging in there now that they're maybe waiting on us.'

'Let's see how many there are in there,' Clem said.

'How we gonna do that?' Bart said, looking askance at Clem.

'Easy.'

Clem grabbed a rock in his left hand and hurled it at a window. He missed.

'You throw like a girl,' Bart said.

'I ain't left handed, dammit. You try.'

Bart selected another rock and threw it.

He didn't miss.

The rear window shattered and the two men waited.

They didn't have to wait long.

Mick O'Hara showed himself briefly at the window.

The flash of his handgun ruined the night vision

of the two men as they stared at the window. They lay flat on the ground and the shot passed harmlessly overhead and thudded into a building behind them sending splinters of wood flying through the air. Sheriff Prady raced to the back of the surgery to find Mick on his haunches, his gun still smoking.

'See anything?' the sheriff asked.

'Nary a thing,' Mick replied. 'Just a rock come flying through the window.'

'Seems they're comin' at us from both directions,' Prady said.

'You seen Sharper?' Mick asked.

'Not yet,' the sheriff replied. 'Not yet.'

CHAPTER 11

Sharper was waiting for the next move when he heard the muffled shot. Damn! he thought, the other two must be at the back of the surgery. He was in a quandary now; should he deal with whoever was shooting at him, or make a tactical retreat and go for the other two? He reasoned that, with Bill and Mick already guarding the rear, he'd take out the shooter from where he was.

Crawling on his belly, he made his way to the nearest building and, slowly rising, leaned against the clapboard wall. Crouching slightly, he peered round the corner of the building in the hope of spotting the shooter. Almost immediately a shot rang out and thudded into the wall above his head. Sharper was showered in wood splinters as he ducked even further, but he'd seen the muzzle flash and now pinpointed his adversary. He moved away from the corner of the building and stealthily made his way round the side to come out behind the man shooting at him.

But Ben Doyle was no slouch when it came to gunplay; he'd already made his next move. Keeping tight against buildings, he crept towards where he'd seen the man he was after, knowing instinctively that the man would have moved. Both men were now trying to outflank each other in a game of cat and mouse.

Without warning, the clouds parted and the moon shone in all its glory, lighting up once-dark alleyways, bright enough to cast shadows. Sharper emerged from the rear of building just as Ben slipped out of the alley but all Sharper caught sight of was the moon reflecting off a spur as its owner disappeared.

Ben waited, straining his ears for any sound, as did Sharper. There seemed to be an impasse. As quickly as the moonlight came, it disappeared as clouds scudded across the sky, obscuring it once more.

Sharper made his move.

'Ain't no need for silence now,' Bart remarked. 'Damn fool Doyle has ruined any advantage we might have had.'

'Let's get this over with,' Clem said. 'I can shoot with my left hand.'

'OK, let's do it!'

Both men opened up simultaneously, peppering the surgery with slugs. The noise was deafening and sulphur filled the air. Reloading, they kept up a fusillade of shots, splintering the wood-framed building and shattering the remaining windows.

In a lull in the shooting, Bill and Mick opened up, firing off rapid shots in the general direction of their attackers. They pulled back once more as the firing opened up again. They were biding their time.

Sharper was alarmed at the shooting he could hear behind him and only hoped Bill and Mick could cope. He quickly fired off two shots and ran across the alley to where he'd seen the spur in the moonlight. Reloading, he fired blindly round the corner of the building before diving to ground as fire was returned.

At last Sharper could see the man as he darted behind a wall. Holding his breath and gently squeezing the trigger, Sharper aimed for the very corner of the building knowing, with any luck, that the bullet would pass through the flimsy wooden wall. He fired off three shots, each slug passing into the wall no more than half an inch apart.

A low groan confirmed his assumption: he'd hit the man. But how badly?

He waited, but no shots were returned. Standing, his Smith & Wesson levelled and cocked, he moved towards the end of the alley. As he

143

neared the corner, he caught sight of a spurred boot. The man was lying flat on his back, his Colt still in his hand and his eyes wide open. Even in the dim light, Sharper could see two holes in the man's chest. Blood was already pooling around the body.

'You!' the man croaked. 'I – I shoulda – killed you when – I had – the chance,' he managed to say as he feebly raised his gun arm.

'Don't even think about it!' Sharper ordered and pulled off his fake beard.

Ben Doyle gasped. 'You!' Ben knew he was a dead man and had nothing to lose. As he tried to squeeze the trigger, Sharper, with his gun already aimed at the prostrate figure, fired. Doyle's body buckled and shuddered as the heavy slug hit him and, in reflex, his Colt fired harmlessly into the air. Sharper wasted no time on the dead man; he figured he got what he deserved.

Now for the other two. If he could position himself, assuming the men hadn't got into the surgery, he might be able to create a crossfire. Hurriedly, he reloaded his handgun and, on impulse, picked up the dead man's Colt. Loading it, he put it in his own holster. He rued leaving the Winchester leaning up against a wall when he was staking out Whittaker's office, but it was too late for recriminations now.

Sharper entered Main Street almost directly

144

opposite the surgery. In the glow of the street lights, he could see the shattered front window and, looking up and down the street, noticed that it was eerily empty. No lights showed in any of the buildings as folks kept to themselves and out of harm's way.

Crossing the street in a low crouch, he headed a block up from the surgery and entered a narrow alleyway, following it to the rear of the buildings. He stopped as he reached the corner of the adjacent building to Doc James's place and slowly peered round the corner.

The firing had been constant from both sides now and the sulphur-filled air was heavy and cloying. Sharper could see where the two men were positioned and took aim. His slug passed overhead but Bart threw himself to the ground.

'Goddamn! Someone's a-shootin' at us from over there,' he pointed to his left.

Clem fired off a useless shot in the general direction and Sharper, seeing muzzle flash, fired back. His slug caught Bart on the left shoulder, tossing him over and backwards with the force of the impact. Bart gave out a scream like a banshee as he hit the ground. That was all the encouragement Bill and Mick needed. They redoubled their efforts, firing as quickly as their guns would allow and, now joined by Abe, they outnumbered the killers by four to one.

Clem could see no point in staying put, especially with only one good arm. He began to crawl away and, passing the prone Bart on the way, he whispered, 'Come on, let's get out of here!'

Bart was in too much pain to answer and the effort required to move at all was all but impossible.

'I ain't hangin' around, Bart, move your sorry ass!' Clem whispered in a hoarse voice.

'I – I cain't move, Clem. Ya gotta help me!' Bart implored.

Clem ignored the plea and continued to crawl, leaving Bart to fend for himself.

'You low down, stinkin' b—' was all Bart got out. As he raised himself up to shout at Clem, a slug took the top of his head off. Blood, gore and bone showered Clem as he tried to move away. He had to get clear before the men rushed him. Deep inside he knew he was doomed.

Bill Prady was the first man out, followed by Mick and Abe, their guns still blazing a trail of death. Clem turned and started to fire back, but he was now in Sharper's line of fire. Sharper didn't hesitate and let loose a carefully aimed shot.

Clem's body buckled like straw in the wind as the slug caught him high up in the chest. In his death throes, his left hand contracted and the Colt exploded a final shot. The bullet caught Sheriff Prady in the leg, thigh high, and, wincing in both pain and shock, he fell to the ground clutching at his wound.

Sharper joined the trio after making sure both men were dead. 'You hit bad, Bill?' he asked.

'Nah, flesh mainly, but sure stings a mite,' the sheriff replied. 'Just a lucky shot, I guess,' he added, with a pained look on his face.

'We got 'em, Sharper,' Mick said excitedly.

'You'll find the third man in an alley opposite,' Sharper said.

'He dead too?' Abe asked.

' 'Fraid so. I had no choice in the matter,' Sharper said.

'That's the end of that, then,' Mick said.

'Not quite,' Sharper replied. 'Not quite.'

All three men looked at him with quizzical expressions on their faces.

'I still got some business to settle,' Sharper said.

He retrieved his Smith & Wesson, slowly reloaded and holstered it, straightened his Stetson and strode off.

'Where ya goin'?' Bill called after him as Doc James ventured outside.

'If Arnie's up to it, Doc,' Sharper said, 'maybe he could take a look at these fellas an' see if they're the ones he saw out at the diggin's.'

'He's doing fine, Sharper. I'll tend Bill's leg first and then help Arnie out here,' the doc replied, and disappeared back inside the surgery to get his black bag.

'These are the men that killed Soo Lee and her grandfather,' Sharper said.

'You sure?' Prady asked.

'Sure as eggs is eggs, Bill.'

Bill asked again: 'Where're ya goin', Sharper?'

'After Whittaker,' was all Sharper said.

CHAPTER 12

Sharper made his way to the livery stables. King snorted, almost angrily, showing he was none too pleased at being left alone for so long. 'Sorry, old buddy,' Sharper soothed, holding a handful of oats to King's muzzle. 'Had some business to settle.' King didn't acknowledge the soothing tones, but lapped up the oats greedily.

Sharper dusted off his saddle, something he would never have had to do if ol' Sam were still here. He'd make sure Arnie kept it spotless now the old man was gone. He saddled up. Half-filling a bucket with water, he allowed King a drink. 'Got us some riding to do, boy,' he said, stroking the animal's neck as he spoke. This time, having drunk the water, King gently nudged his master: a sign of forgiveness. Sharper finished dressing King; having put the bridle and bit on and pulled the reins over King's head, he mounted.

He knew he could take his time. The fat lawyer was hardly a force to be reckoned with and the buggy would be easy to track down. He walked King to the front of Whittaker's office first. He retrieved the Winchester and set that in his saddle-boot, then walked King to the rear of the office. He picked up the distinctive wheel ruts and walked on at a steady pace, following them.

At the edge of town, the tracks led up into the foothills following the old trail. Sharper gave a small grin as he thought there was no way a buggy could make it all the way to the top. Reining in King, he rolled a cigarette and drew deeply. He exhaled and felt himself calm down. Sharper was not a killer. Yes, he'd killed many men in his time, but never through choice and even now his conscience still pricked at him.

He sat awhile, looking at the sky, which was clearing rapidly, allowing the moon and a myriad of stars to shine down. How many times, he thought, had he marvelled at a night-time sky? Smoking leisurely, he stroked King's mane and revelled in the peace and quiet of the open air. He finished his cigarette and stubbed the burning end between thumb and forefinger to make sure it was out, before tossing it to one side. 'Let's ride, boy,' he said to King and, without having to spur the animal on, the Arab started to walk again.

*

Back in town, folks began to emerge from the safety of their homes and businesses as the shooting stopped. Mutterings and rumours were rife as they tried to guess what had gone on.

Doc James had bound Sheriff Prady's leg and given him a small dose of laudanum to ease the pain and a wooden crutch to help him move. Prady was in full command now as his office dictated. He ordered some men to bring all three bodies to the front of the surgery building and lay them, side by side, on the boardwalk. He instructed another townsman to go get Barney, the undertaker, and asked Doc James if he could fetch young Arnie out. A few moments later, Arnie, helped by the doc, stepped on to the boardwalk. Although still weak and in some pain, the boy's eyes were bright with excitement as he faced the milling throng.

'Arnie, I want you to be sure, now,' the sheriff began. 'You recognize any of these fellas?'

Arnie took a step towards the three bodies and studied their faces for a moment before saying, 'I sure do, Sheriff. Them's the ones I saw kill those old prospectors up in the foothills.'

'You sure, Arnie?' the sheriff pressed.

'Yes, sir,' Arnie replied.

'Sharper has already stated that these are the men who killed Soo and Chen Lee,' continued the sheriff.

The small group of Chinese men nodded and chatted away in their own language before one stepped forward and thanked the lawman.

'No need to thank me,' Prady said. 'Sharper Wade's the man to thank; he's the one who chased these men down.'

Barney arrived on his funeral wagon, shrouds at the ready, and was quickly followed by Mark Twain and a photographer from the *Territorial Enterprise*, who had come to record the scene for posterity.

The buggy tracks were easy to follow; obviously Whittaker hadn't been expecting anyone to follow him out here, but where was he going and why? And, for that matter, where the hell had Silas Marsh disappeared to?

The trail began to rise now, becoming stonier and rougher as nature fought to take over what was rightfully hers. King walked on, carefully picking his way through the rough terrain, Sharper trusting his every move.

Lance Whittaker had reached the rock crevice and stood, wiping his sweat-soaked brow as he waited for his partners in crime to join him and dispose of the body. His hands were shaking, both from nerves and the buggy ride. He reached into his top pocket and pulled out a cigar. Lighting up, he inhaled deeply – too deeply as it happened and began to cough loudly.

Cursing himself for not bringing any of his favourite imported whisky, he took a swig from his canteen. The tepid and brackish-tasting water eased his throat some and he leaned against the buggy and tried to calm his over-stretched nerves. The plan had to work. Had to! Not only was his livelihood and position – such as it was – at stake but also his life. Involuntarily, his hand moved up to his throat as he imagined the noose tightening and his body suspended at the end of a rope. He shuddered and, more than ever, wanted that whisky. He drew on his cigar again, this time not too deeply, and glanced at the rolled-up Indian rug containing the man he had killed.

The sound of the raucous coughing was picked up by King before Sharper heard it. King's ears pricked up and Sharper knew he'd heard something. Then the noise filtered through to him. Sharper smiled. So he was close. He nudged King onwards and continued up the gentle climb, again. No need to rush; his prey wasn't going anywhere. As a precaution, he double-checked his handgun; it was fully loaded.

Sharper knew where the man would be now: in the rock crevice, waiting for the three killers. Three killers who would never make it. He was no more than a hundred yards away now, so he decided to dismount and approach on foot. He loosely hitched King to a cactus and stroked the animal's neck saying, 'Be back real soon, partner.'

Taking out his handgun, he then walked along the trail until he reached the crevice. Peering round, he saw the buggy, with Lance Whittaker nervously pacing to and fro, the cigar end red against the black rock wall. Sharper re-holstered his gun and walked into the crevice.

Whittaker saw movement but it was too dark to make out who it was. 'That you, Bart?' he called out.

There was no reply.

'Clem? Ben?' Panic was now rising in Whittaker's throat. 'Who is it?'

Sharper neared and said, in a low, menacing voice. 'Your worst nightmare, Whittaker.'

The cigar fell limply from Whittaker's fingers as he recognized Sharper Wade. Fumbling, with nothing now to lose, he went for his gun. But Sharper could have whistled Dixie and drawn faster than him.

But Sharper wasn't shooting to kill. He wanted this man to hang.

The slug caught Whittaker in the arm, forcing him to drop the half-drawn side iron. He howled like a girl as the pain hit him. Sharper holstered his Smith & Wesson and calmly walked towards the fat lawyer. As he reached the buggy, he saw the Indian rug.

'Well, well, what have we got here?' Sharper said. He hefted the rug to the ground and revealed the body of Silas Marsh, already stiff and beginning to smell as bodily fluids found their way out of the dead deputy. 'So that leaves just you, Whittaker and sure as hell, you'll swing for this,' Sharper said.

He wrapped the body up again and placed it back on the buggy. He whistled and King pulled his reins free of the cactus and entered the crevice. 'Good boy,' Sharper said as he took his lariat from the saddle horn.

Whittaker was whimpering, clutching his arm as Sharper tied him up and frog-marched him to the buggy. Tying King to the buggy, too, Sharper headed back into town.

Dawn saw Prady, a tough old *hombre*, atop his horse leading a small party of men, including Arnie, to the diggings where Arnie had seen the killings. Arriving there, Arnie led the sheriff to the crest of the ridge and pointed down. Prady slid his Stetson back on his head and whistled. Even from this height he could see at least a dozen bodies down there in various stages of decomposition, some still being attacked by buzzards.

It took a few hours to get enough volunteers and buckboards to take the rocky trail down into the canyon. Barney Gilpin led the team with his funeral buggy, a whole mess of shrouds loaded in the back.

The smell hit the party long before the sight of the bodies. Buzzards rose, squawking in their anger at being disturbed from a feast they'd claimed as their own. Many of the bodies were mere skeletons, partly covered in torn and tattered clothing; others still had a vestige of flesh on their bones.

None were recognizable.

Whittaker was unceremoniously dumped off at the sheriff's office and Doc James reluctantly, and none too gently, fixed up the whimpering lawyer's arm. Sharper, accompanied by a limping Sheriff Prady, returned to the hotel he had yet to spend a night in. Dog-tired as he was, he was also in need of a drink. It was early, though, and the saloon was closed, but the hotel had a small bar and Prady ordered the desk clerk to open up and serve them. Under protest, the man did as ordered. 'Leave the bottle,' Prady said.

'Who's paying for this?' the snooty man asked, looking down his sharp, bird-like nose at Sharper, who was covered in trail dust and smelled none too sweet.

'The town is,' Prady answered.

'Hmm,' the man replied and walked off.

'If I had the energy,' Sharper said, 'I'd smooth

that jackal's nose out some.'

Prady grinned. 'Accidents do happen,' he said as he filled the shot glasses. 'The judge has been informed,' Prady went on. 'Trial's in the morning, and with you and Arnie as witnesses, Whittaker will hang for sure.'

'Even that's too good for that varmint,' Sharper said as he sank the whiskey in one go.

'I coulda sworn you'd'a killed him,' Prady said.

'Believe me, I wanted to, but I wanted justice to take its course.' Sharper leaned forward and filled the glasses again. 'I gotta get me some sleep, Bill,' he said eventually. 'I'll call in later this afternoon and make a statement, OK?'

'Sure, I'll be there,' Prady said.

Shaking hands, the two men parted.

CHAPTER 13

The trial, as expected, was short-lived.

The testimonies of Arnie and Sharper, coupled with documents and almost fifteen thousand dollars worth of gold recovered from Whittaker's office, condemned the fat man to a necktie party. The judge deliberated for only a few moments after the jury returned a unanimous guilty verdict, before he announced the death penalty. The court erupted into cheers and clapping that no amount of gavel-banging would stop.

Once outside, Sharper decided it was time to move on. His departure, however was delayed by a group of Chinese men and women, friends and relatives of Soo and Chan Lee who were there to pay their respects to the man who had avenged the killings. They came armed with fruit, cakes, chunks of meat and whiskey as gifts to show their gratitude.

For the first time in his life, Sharper was embarrassed by all the attention and adulation he was receiving, and thanked the people for their generosity. When they departed, he said to Prady, 'Can you give this to the needy? All except the whiskey,' he grinned.

'Sure thing, Sharper. You sure you won't change your mind and stay on a while?'

'I gotta keep moving, Bill. I been here too long as it is. I miss the open trail. I'm just a drifter.'

Prady shook his hand. 'Well if you're ever back in this part of the world—'

'Sure, I'll make sure I pay you a visit.'

Arnie came out of the court with a smile wider than the Mississippi. 'Mr Prady, Mr Sharper, Sam left me the livery and whole mess of money!'

'Good for you, Arnie, you'll make a fine livery-man,' Sharper said. 'Now, I must be heading off,' he added.

Arnie held his hand out and Sharper took it. 'You take care, kid.'

'I will, Mr Sharper. I will.'

Mounting up, Sharper waved once and headed out of Virginia City. Not once did he turn round.

'There rides a fine man,' Prady said to no one in particular. 'Sorry to see him go.' Prady turned on his heel and walked back to his office.

The three killers, along with Silas Marsh, were buried in unmarked graves in Boot Hill.

No one attended.

Back in his office, all Prady could hear was the whimpering noises made by Lance Whittaker, the architect of this whole mess, as he knew his visualization of the noose around his neck was about to come true.